WAG & SCALLY

in
White House Skuldoggery

BARON VON DENNIS

BLUE SUN BOOKS

PREVIOUS UNPUBLISHED BOOKS BY
BARON VON DENNIS

'Love in the Age of the Coronavirus'

'The Rebellion of the Bengali Birdwatchers' (Sylvia Shyte
Series 1)

'Dead Shoes Don't Walk Upon Water, Mister'

'Janus, the Two-Headed Dog-Fearing Monkey Detective'

'Attack of the Tattooed Fallen Angels from Betelgeuse'

'Zombie Babies Die Hard'

'The Man who Ate a Dictionary & Lived to Tell a Thousand
Tales' (also available in versions of Finnish, Esperanto
& Latin dictionaries)

'The Unemployed Workers' Rights to More Free Time'
(A Self-Help Manual)

CONTENTS

CHAPTER ONE

When Queenie Calls

SOMEWHERE in the urban streets of Britdog there lurked a dark menace…

There is an eerie *psspllllpp* sound that only the most astute dog ears can pick up. Is that a figure crouching in the darkness near a wall or the shadow of a shadow?

"Wag, are you doing your doggy business right in front of the ATM machine again?"
A black spaniel with large floppy ears trotted out from the dark night.
"Sure thing, Scally. Money's a terrible business and you got to step into poop to get your paws dirty with it these days."

Scally shook his little hairy head and rubbed at a small stain on his crimson waistcoat. "You're a downright revolutionary, Wag."

Wag sat down, leaned back, and sniffed his rump. "We're all born revolutionaries, Scally. Just that most get it trained out of them."

"Well, get your revolutionary ass back in the shadows - we're still on stake-out here."

Wag scampered over to behind the tree where his companion, Scally, was crouched. If there was ever a pooch who could sniff out a catch, it was Scally. As a Yorkshire terrier he was a razor-sharp hunting dog with a wit to match the keenest minds of the canine age. Scally's ears pricked up and he instinctively leaned forward with his left paw off the ground. It was a natural instinctual position before lurching.

The doors of the bank burst open and two bulky shapes dashed out. They each had a large sack over their shoulders. They dumped the sacks into the back of a nearby pick-up truck and scrabbled into the front seats.

"Grok'em," hissed Scally under his breath as he crept out and ran towards the back of the pick-up truck keeping low to the ground. Wag followed behind. He was naturally a low-ground kind of guy. His belly was never far from the ground regardless of running, walking, or doing his doggy business.

Wag and Scally just managed to jump up and over and tumble under the canvas cover at the back of the pick-up before it sped off into the deepest dark of a damn dark night. If there was a moon, she was sleeping.

Wag grimaced. "I'm being tossed around like a dog-damn omelet." It was true. The truck was rocking around as it tumbled through the streets. Wag was trying his best to hold on to the sides. A spotlight suddenly lit up Scally's face. Wag fell back.

"Whooh, Scally. Stop scaring the cats outta me."

Scally grinned as he shone the torch in Wag's face. "Time to let the air out of these guys' fun." He reached inside his waistcoat and brought out a thick metallic-looking object.

"An electric can opener?"

"Come on, rumphead, I don't carry that stuff on chases with me. This is my Swiss Dogknife. With it I can cut my paw nails, open a can of food, and… slash some tires."

Wag nodded. "Impressive kit. Someone's been bargain hunting at the Dog Army Stores recently."

"Grab hold of my back paws!" Scally opened the side of the canvas covering and slipped out. Wag leaned forward and grabbed onto Scally's hind legs with all his spaniel strength. It always worried him when Scally did his dare-doggy tricks. A few seconds later and something between a squeal, a swerve, a shaggy-dog storm, and a sewage-dog shriek erupted at the same time. The truck lurched from side to side a couple of times, throwing Wag up and down and hitting his head against the metal side. But Wag wouldn't let go of his buddy. He continued to squeeze tightly as he felt his world rumble-tumble and tip over. The truck must have hit a curb as it suddenly flipped onto its side. An awful screech of metal against concrete lasted for enough seconds to deafen a choir of drunken night cats. When the truck had come to a halt, Wag opened his eyes to find he was holding onto nothing, and Scally was nowhere to be found. Wag hurriedly scrambled out of the back and onto the now lopsided roof of the vehicle. He was slightly dazed but certainly not out of the game. Then Wag saw what looked to be a St. Bernard stagger out of the truck and try to make a dash for it. Yet before the St. Bernard could get to the bushes across the road he slumped into a heap. Wag turned to see Scally standing coolly in the middle of the road with a blow-dart in his mouth. Scally gave the paw-thumbs up. Then another St. Bernard started crawling out of the driver's side door, only to have Wag jump down onto its back.

"Come on, you Boris!" Wag was standing on his hind back legs as if surfing the dazed St. Bernard. The large brute fell on its side and stared up at Wag who, unceremoniously, ripped the barrel away from the dog's collar, pulled out the cork with his teeth, and took a long drag. "Puhh! Ah, damn brandy. Don't you St. Bernards ever carry any decent stuff in your barrels?"

The large dog snarled and tried to get up.

Wag whipped out his favorite tool – the tazer. "Now, how many have I tazed today – one, two, three? Perhaps four? I bet you're thinking I got no more tazing juice in this here tazer. Well, do you wanna try it, Boris, or not? Come on punk, go for it – make my day."

The St. Bernard was exhausted but still managed to growl. "My name's not Boris," he said in a deep voice, "it's Cedric."

"No skin off my paws. All dippy St. Bernards are Borises in my book. So, Boris-punk – you feeling lucky? Are you?"

A dart whistled into the side of the St. Bernard and the large dog slumped forward.

Wag turned around. "Hey, I hadn't finished with this Boris. Why did you have to stun dart him?"

"Wag, come on, drop it with the *feeling lucky punk* routine – it's getting old."

Wag grinned. It was still his favorite routine.

Scally pulled out his mobile phone and made a call. "I'm calling in the clean-up guys," he said over to Wag. "No point in us breaking a sweat trying to haul these damn St. Bernards in."

Wag took another swig from the brandy

barrel he had reclaimed. "Yup. It's not for us to lump around these Borises – damn heavy doggy dudes. And about as clever as a corrupt politician."

Scally looked over. "A corrupt politician? I think you'll find that's a tautology, like saying water is wet."

Wag shrugged. "Taught or not taught – it's true in my book."

Scally nodded in agreement. It had been a long night.

After a few hours rest, Wag and Scally were back at home and sitting around the breakfast table. Scally was looking over the day's news, scrolling his paws over the tablet whilst sipping on his strong, black coffee. Wag was leaning back on the last two legs of the chair, throwing crunchies into the air and catching them in his mouth. "Life ain't a box of chocolates – that's the dumbest thing I've ever heard. Life is more like an endless stream of dog crunchies."

Scally ignored him. Then the phone rang. He picked it up. "Yes. Yes. Yes. Confirmed." He put the phone down and continued sipping his coffee.

Wag scratched his belly. "One of your secret lovers?" he asked, trying to sound disinterested.

"Nope. We have an emergency, top secret, urgent meeting with the boss over at Dog Intelligence HQ."

Wag tossed another crunchie into the air. "No rush then."

Scally sipped his coffee. "Nope."

SOME time later at a secret location…

The elevator doors opened, and the armed dog guard nodded to Wag and Scally. They exited into a long corridor, at the end of which was a large arched door. Above, it read – **Dog Intelligence 1.**

Wag looked up. "I never could figure out why they didn't just call it Dog Intelligence instead of Dog Intelligence 1?"

"I think the web URL for Dog Intelligence was already taken." Scally stroked his nose and straightened his newly cleaned crimson waistcoat. "Ready, Wag? Go easy on the revolutionary dogma this time."

They entered the office and Scally suavely strolled over to the desk where an elegantly dressed and very attractive Pomeranian dog was sitting at her computer. She looked up and pulled down her black-rimmed spectacles.

"Hello Scally – you're late, as always."

Scally twitched his little Yorkshire terrier nose. "My dear Epiphany, punctuality is for cretins. Why be on time when the world waits for you and me?"

The lady Epiphany smiled. "Your time is your own world, Scally. And there's only room for you and your pal, Wag." She looked over at Wag. "No offense."

Wag shrugged. "None taken. The system commodifies us all anyway. We're all exploited."

Scally frowned at Wag before turning his attention back to Epiphany. "Darling, there is always room in my world for a genius such as yourself."

Epiphany smiled. "Maybe, Scally. Keep working on it. But first, the boss – *W* – wants to see you both. She's been kept waiting and she's not well-plug pleased."

They all grinned. It was their private joke, for the boss, *W*, was a pug. And, as Scally liked to whisper under his doggy breath – this one pug was both smart and smug. Scally shot Epiphany one of his best 'scally' looks before being buzzed into the main head office.

"Stop looking smug!" growled a bad-tempered pug.
"Hello *W*," replied Scally cheerily.
Wag held up a paw but said nothing.
W sat back in her highchair behind the large oak desk. It had to be a highchair otherwise she would not reach the top of the desk.
"You were expected over an hour ago. What in the dog-races do you think we do here – play monopoly? This is the dog-damn head of the

nation's intelligence services. We're the ones who keep our country – United Kingdog – safe from harm. You got that?"

Scally scratched his hairy chin. "Have you seen the dog-traffic out there, *W*? You've got to do something with all the new automated *Duber-Dog* taxis – they're clogging up all the lanes."

W scowled. "Take the metro."

"Full of street dogs," sniffed Scally.

Wag shook his head and sighed.

"So, what's the urgency, boss? We got another criminal gang of dog-hackers stealing from the government again?"

Wag raised a paw in solidarity, but out of sight of *W*'s view.

W heaved a big sigh. "This one's not on our turf, Scally. But it's a request that comes from her Majesty."

Scally's ears perked up. "From Queenie?"

W nodded with her round, puggish face. "Sit down and watch this." She pressed a button on her desk and a large screen came down from the ceiling. Scally and Wag sat back and watched as the face of a regal corgi appeared, decked in a diamond collar.

"Dear defenders of our beloved United Kingdog, your majesty has a royal-dog request of you." Queenie's voice was serious as she spoke in her established clear diction – or what Wag would simply call *posh*. "I have just recently received a very distressing call from our cousins over the pond. Our sister nation, United States of Ameridog, is under grave threat. Their Presidog, Frumpus, called me in a state of great agitation. He needs our help if the sovereignty of the United States of Ameridog is to be upheld. It seems there is a dastardly dog-plot from another nation to intervene in the political affairs of the country. This could very well be a new form of dog-warfare. We cannot allow the political system of our dear cousins to be brought down like this. Besides, it would reflect badly on us." Queenie made a little cough, and she brought her gloved corgi paw to her mouth. "I have asked our head of Dog Intelligence – *W* – to put our best agents on the case. If you are watching this now, then this means you. Go now to our cousins and show them the United Kingdog spirit – save them from peril."

Queenie coughed again then looked off to the side. Not realizing the camera was still rolling, she called out to one of her aides – *where is my damned son Barlie, that good-for-nothing Basset Hound? Is he still sniffing around in the bushes? That dog-boy had better buckle up his ideas soon or he's out of a future job…he'll have to farm for a living!*

"Ahem." *W* hurriedly stopped the recording. "So, that's your summons. Queenie wants you both to fly out to Washington first thing. The plane is being fueled as I speak. Pavlov, our trusted science director, will kit you out with all the stuff you need."

Scally sniffed casually. "Looks like the dog-dudes of Ameridog have a problem. What is it this time – have they run out of tofu hamburgers?"

W pulled one of her unimpressed puggish faces. "Not a time to be a cocky spaniel, Scally. This time it appears serious. It's got Queenie all wound-up."

Oh, a wound-up corgi, thought Wag - but he was wise enough not to say anything.

"And if our Queenie is troubled," continued W, 'then that makes trouble for us. And I don't like that kind of trouble around here. Get your paws over the pond and sort this mess out so we can go back to reading the papers. Oh, and another thing – be careful over there both of you. It's a wild, wild country.'

Scally flicked a speck of fluff from his waistcoat. "Don't worry, boss – we'll get this case cracked in the Wag and Scally way. And we'll show those yanky-doodle dogs a trick or two."

W sighed. "That's what I fear. Just don't post anything on social media this time. And be discreet - if you possibly can! Best of doggy luck to you both. I have a feeling you're going to need it."
Scally gave the paws up.

We don't need luck, thought Wag – what we need is
a revolution.

In the outer office, Epiphany beckoned Wag and
Scally over to her desk.

"I don't like the sound of this mission. I've
seen some of the documents. Frumpus seems to be
in real trouble – and he may take you down with
him. There's a lot of rogues over there in Washington.
Trust no dog. If they don't smell right, stay well clear!
Take care, the both of you."

Scally stroked the hair down around his nose.
"Don't worry – I'll be back for that doggy-date with
you, Epiphany. No one messes with Wag and Scally.
Least of all a bunch of untrained cowdogs." Scally
gave a wink and strolled to the door.

Wag held up his paw. "Down with the
globalists – power to the dog paws!"

Back in the elevator, the dog guard pressed the
button for the basement to take them to the science –
or cool gadgetry – department.

"Why is it always the revolutionary stuff
when we come here, Wag?" Scally shook his furry
head.

Wag shrugged. "They hate it. That means I
enjoy it."

"I think you're more of a mime artist than a
Marxist."

Wag grinned. "You got your ways, I have mine."

"Sure thing, Wag – sure thing. Anyhow, let's get our gear from Pavlov and hit that plane."

The elevator came to a halt. No one moved. There was an uncomfortable few seconds of silence.

CHAPTER TWO

Wag & Scally go to Washington

Wag leaned back in his plane seat with his little feet dangling over the arm rest. He swigged from a small bottle and licked his lips. Wag had an unmissable long tongue, almost twice as long as his floppy spaniel ears.

Scally was reclining in his seat reading a book. The small private jet was exclusively for 'espionage' use only and had transported some of the best spy-dogs in the recent history of Dog Intelligence.

Wag licked around the top of the empty bottle. "Why are the bottles on planes always so small? I mean, we don't get smaller when we fly, so why should the bottles?" He reached around in front of him to find more of the bottles, and some snacks.

"Google it, Wag – why don't you search it to find out?"

"What? And give those capitalist titans my private digital data – no thanks, matey! I'm not going to be a pawn in their surveillance capitalism game."

"Wag, you're forgetting we're spies. We always go dark web – we don't do surface web. That's for the monkeys."

Wag nodded. "Good point." He looked over at Scally who was leafing through a thick book. "What's your plane read – it looks like an encyclopedia?"

"It's called *The Singularity is Near*, by this dog dude Roy Rockweil."

"Is it near?"

"Is what?"

"The singularity." Wag threw another empty bottle onto the floor.

"I think Rockweil is anti-dog. He thinks we're all going to upload our dog minds into a digital-dog cloud."

"Freak me! How are we going to pee on the famous statues if our minds are in the dog-cloud?"

"That's the point, Wag – we'll all be controlled in some unified dog-collective."

Wag rubbed his belly with both paws. "Sounds like cat poo to me." He put the blinkers over his eyes and rolled over. "Wake me up when we land, not before. I need my beauty sleep."

Scally got out the 'Top Secret' file he had been given by *W* just before leaving. He opened it and looked at a picture of a white poodle with a mop of frizzy hair. Underneath the picture it read – '*Frumpus*, 45th Presidog of the United States of Ameridog. Not sure if his breed origin is Germany or France.' Underneath that it listed the Presidog's closest aides.

Spencer - Vicedog of Washington – an ex-military Labrador breed with short-cut hair. Regarded as faithful and loyal to the Presidog.

Podenko – Captain of US Presidog Guards – a German Shephard hunting dog. Especially decorated for his bravery in hunting in packs. Currently regarded as loyal to the Presidog.

Ayewanna – ex-wife of Presidog *Frumpus*. She is a Cesky Fousek. She displays lots of energy, is regarded as frivolous, and not particularly friendly with other dogs. She is to be considered more of a nuisance than a danger. It seems she is now seeking to exploit the Presidog's recent affair with *Sueme*.

Sueme – an attractive and seductive Siamese cat. Due to a recent leak to the press, it was revealed that she is a 'female companion' of the Presidog. This is now causing a great political scandal for Frumpus. This may be regarded as a deliberate act of sabotage, known as a 'honey trap.' *Sueme* is to be considered an 'unknown entity' and should be handled with care.

QA – a highly secret organization based around the current Presidog. Allegedly made up from the highest military personnel as well as high-ranking politicians and 'dogs of influence' and other social-political VIDs (Very Important Dogs). This organization is alleged to have a mandate to protect the true sovereignty of the United States of Ameridog. It is highly connected, well-organized, and is rumored to be operative within many networks of power. More must be known about **QA**!

Scally closed the file. He thought to himself: that's interesting - illicit relations between a Presidog and a Siamese cat. Well, that's a first. I must get to the bottom of that little affair…if I have time. Scally was suspicious of cats. More than that, he was suspicious of how cats thought. He couldn't always read what they were thinking. The working of their minds alluded him, most of the time, and that annoyed Scally more than he cared to admit. He couldn't quite imagine how a dog would have a cat lover. Maybe it's platonic, he wondered.

Scally was still scheming in this mind when the private jet landed at a small airport near to the capital. Good, thought Scally, at least no queuing. Wag and Scally arrived in the United States of Ameridog on diplomatic immunity. After all, it had been Frumpus himself who had invited them. And as Wag and Scally saw it, they were here to clear up his doggy do-do. They walked through the almost empty private airport.

"Looks like this is where the VIDs enter the country. No customs here," said Scally to Wag as they strolled to collect their luggage.

"And the drugs, too," replied Wag.

"Don't be silly," responded Scally, "the United States of Ameridog doesn't ship in their own drugs." Then they both burst out into doggy laughter. Sarcasm was one of their favorite forms of export.

As they reached the main doors a burly security guard jumped out in front of them. He was armed to the teeth with guns and weapons and the usual paraphernalia.

"What you guys got in your bags," growled the over-sized Rottweiler.

Scally looked at Wag and Wag shrugged.

"Guys, I need to know what's in your bags,"repeated the security guard.

"Ammunition, guns, surface-to-air missiles, poisoned liquor, deadly snake venom, and replacement underwear. The usual diplomatic stuff," answered Wag in a deadpan voice.

"You guys kidding me?!" barked the Rottweiler.

"We don't kid," responded Scally, "were dog-dead serious. Now out of our way, you diaper-wearing dog child."

The security guard was stunned into silence. Then just as he was about to draw his pistol...

"Ah, wonderful, our guests are here! Come, gentlemen, our illustrious Presidog Frumpus is awaiting your presence. I am your contact, McMurphy." An imposing Irish wolfhound in a chauffeur's uniform stepped forward. "It's okay, Danny, these gentlemen are the guests of the state. They have full immunity."

The security Rottweiler grumbled and stepped back. He obviously recognized the authority of McMurphy. Scally gave a smile to Danny, the guard, and followed the chauffeur.

Wag stuck up his paw. "Kiss my revolution, Danny boy!"

As they were leaving, Scally noticed a couple of shadowy figures lurking in the background. He quickly managed to squeeze his waistcoat collar to activate the hidden camera. He didn't like suspicious activity – not on his watch.

A few minutes later and they were whizzing down the freeway in the back of a black limousine. The freeway was six-lanes and full of cars. McMurphy was cheerful and chatting away in his Irish accent.

"The United States of Ameridog is a big place, boys."

"You don't say?" replied Scally, carefully eyeing the new surroundings.

"Yeah, but don't worry lads, you'll be fine here, I can tell. As they say, in the kingdog of the blind, the one-eyed dog is king." McMurphy laughed and turned on some music. "Mind a bit of *Dog Jovi*? I love this band. These guys are real Ameridogs."

"I'm a *Rage Against the Dogmachine* fan myself," shouted back Wag. "But I'll take your teen pop music if I have to." McMurphy frowned but didn't say anything.

Scally gave Wag a look. "Do you think you can be friendly to the dogs over here?"

Wag shrugged and grabbed a bottle from the limousine's mini bar. "I'll see what I can do. But my thread is short, and my wit is wanting."

Scally observed the passing scenery in silence as the limousine entered the city of Washington and the freeway turned into wide avenues. There were huge buildings everywhere, and the first thing that struck Scally was the number of Ameridog flags hanging from windows and houses. Everything here is big, he thought. Life is lived big here. Big buildings, big food, big cars, big lies, and big secrets. He knew they had to be ready for something different. The uncertain. The unpredictable. They could trust no thing and no dog. The bigger the lie, the more that the dog masses believe it.

McMurphy drove them into an underground car park of an exclusive hotel. As Wag and Scally were walking from the limousine to the subterranean elevator, Scally thought he saw the two shadowy figures again. They were figures dressed in black, lurking just beyond visual contact. The hair rose on the back of Scally's neck. It was not a good sign. Another 'not-so-good-sign' was that they had been assigned a luxury suite in the hotel. Far too luxurious for their breeding.

"I hope we're not supposed to be invisible here in Washington," said Wag with a sarcastic tone. "They've even given us flowers," he noted. "What else – a welcome package to the White House with a door key?"

Scally wasn't impressed either. He picked up a book left lying on the table for guests. *Lives of the Monster Dogs* by Kirsten Barking. Ominous. He frowned.

"Dog-damn ominous, Scally," said Wag, unimpressed.

"Did you notice those dogs-in-black, hanging in the shadows?"

Wag nodded. "Of course. Not much gets past the Wag."

"Did you get a sniff?"

"Yep. Not a scent. Clean."

"Same here. Scentless. Not a drop of glandular pong. That's not normal. It just isn't dog-like."

"I don't like or trust things I can't smell," replied Wag, looking out from the window of the hotel suite. "Think we could survive a fall from here?"

Scally trotted over for a look. "Nah. Doubtful. There's only concrete at the bottom – we'd need a swimming pool at least."

"Damn hairless breeds - they're stitching us up, Scally."

"What's the first Wag and Scally rule?"

"Don't play their doggy game," replied Wag with a grin.

They both took the stairs rather than the elevator. In the Wag and Scally handbook, elevators were trap-boxes. Once inside, you had no place to go. And once the doors opened, you had nowhere to hide your face. Good job they did take the stairs for as soon as they peaked through the small window in the stairwell door of the lobby, they saw them. The two dogs-in-black from before. They were standing in the lobby, keeping watch. One of them had an eye on the elevator whilst the other was observing the revolving door at the entrance.

"Damn these snoopies," muttered Scally. "A decent dog can't go anywhere in this town without being trailed."

Wag saw the opportunity. "Quick, this way." He slipped out the door and jumped onto a passing luggage trolly. Scally swiftly followed. They snook in between the bags of luggage as it was being pulled across the lobby. It stopped at the reception desk. Wag and Scally sprang off and sneaked through an adjacent door. It led into the staff area. As they scampered down an indistinct corridor a receptionist came out of a side door.

"Oh, I'm sorry. This area is private - can I help you?" asked the receptionist in a formal tone.

Without hesitation, Scally whipped out a card from his waistcoat and flashed it in his face. "We're the Cleanliness Inspectors and we're here to inspect your cleanliness."

The receptionist looked surprise. With his sagging dog eyes he looked from Scally to Wag and back to Scally again.

"You better be clean, Man, or we're coming after you," said Wag in a deadpan voice.

"I'm afraid my colleague speaks the truth," added Scally. "Could you point us to your laundry room?"

The receptionist started to stutter.

It didn't take them long to locate the laundry room and get their doggy behinds down the laundry chute that dumped them into a large container. Once outside, they scampered several blocks until they were out of visual sight from the high-class hotel. Now they were happier. The two Britdog agents were more in their element, out on the street, strutting their stuff. This was a new neighborhood and a good opportunity to explore the Washington scene. They rounded a corner and almost walked straight into the chanting crowd. Dogs of all breeds, sizes, and colors were marching in what looked like a protest. Wag and Scally just managed to dodge from colliding into the back of the crowd. They jumped onto the sidewalk as the jeering, chanting crowd scuffled past, holding placards and torn squares of cardboard. Several of the placards had **DLM** scribbled across them.

"Whoa, dudes, what's the hammering about?" called out Wag.

A short-haired female Chihuahua shouted back aggressively – "Get with the program – get woke. Dog Lives Matter...Dog Lives Matter!"

Wag turned to Scally, who looked in a pensive mood. "Get with the program, Scally – get woke."

Scally sighed. "Come on, Wag. Let's keep awake before we get woke." They both quickly exited the street by the nearest side alley. It seemed like the best option until…

…a brute pooch slipped out from the side of the alley and blocked their way. The dude dog was shaggy and tall. He observed them carefully as Wag and Scally approached. They stopped at a stand-off. A few more ruffian fellas slid out from the side shadows of the alley and closed in.

"You're on our patch. And that don't look good, mister," said the main shaggy brute. Scally eyed him over. He looked to be a Great Dane breed. Typical, thought Scally. The Danes are usually good natured when in good health. But when down-and-out, they can be damn nasty.

"I wouldn't think that Ameridog soil would be the neighborhood for a Great Dane either, bro." Scally looked his opponent straight in the eye.

The Great Dane sniffed. "My ancestors came here a long time ago. This is my hood now. And you ain't one of my hoodies. And you ain't my bro, neither. So, little spud, what's your thing?"

Wag looked at Scally and shrugged. Then he pulled out a toothpick and began picking his teeth. "You spudding my pal?" said Wag in a low voice.

The Great Dane came a step closer. "I spud

who I want in my hood. And that includes you too, spud runt."

The Great Dane didn't get to say much else as Wag darted at the Dane and kicked his feet away from under him. The Dane slumped and Wag immediately grabbed his collar and poked him with something in his paw. A huge *buzzzzzzzz* sounded and the Dane shook violently. A smell of burnt hair filled the air.

"Ah, don't taze me, man – don't taze me!" barked the Great Dane desperately.

Scally turned to face the other dogs in the alley that surrounded them. "Back off, minions, or we'll taze your boss til he's hairless," he shouted. The other dogs stepped back. "Wag, do we need to taze this thug again?"

Wag sat on the Great Dane's back and rubbed his chin. "Maybe we should…or maybe we definitely should?"

"Nah, please, back off bro. I ain't doing no harm. It's okay – you can be in ma hood."

"Damn right we can, scuff-ball," replied Wag. "You don't dis a dog dude from the United Kingdog."

"True," added Scally calmly. "It's not good manners." Scally looked them all over. All the dogs seemed brutish but not well-organized. "What do you do around here?"

"What??"The Great Dane still looked dazed.

Wag knocked on his head. "What's ya thing,

man? What's ya hanging at?" Wag thought he was speaking the local lingo, but he wasn't quite sure, and he didn't particularly care either.

"We extort money from this hood, and all the dogs who pass through here," muttered the Great Dane.

"Who for? You're certainly not the top dog here," questioned Scally. The Great Dane appeared reluctant to speak. Wag pushed the tazer into his collar.

"Okay, okay bro, just don't taze me again. We work for the Dogfather."

"The Dogfather?"

"Yeah, he's the head hound of this turf. He's the boss here."

"And which Dogfather is that? There's always more than one."

"Don Columdog."

Scally pulled a card out from the inner pocket of his waistcoat. "Here, give this to your Don Columdog. Let him know it was us who tazed his Dane. And tell him that we're on the same side. We're here to make sure that the White House is for real Ameridogs. We may even call on his assistance one day. We hope he knows which side he's on."

Scally thought it a good thing to make their presence known with the underdog world. After all, it wouldn't be long before the word got around anyway. It was a Wag and Scally policy of facing things head on instead of doggying around and dog-foot dancing away from a situation. As Wag often liked to say – 'you got to look a dog in the face when you're speaking to them.' Otherwise, tazing was always a second option.

A short while later and they were both sitting in a nearby diner named the 'Barking Mad Diner.' They had ordered a couple of hamburgers, one with extra hot chilies.

"These dudes here are pussy cats when it comes to chilies," muttered Wag as he bit into his first burger. The waitress, a golden Labrador, was still standing by the table, hovering around.

"What?" said Wag, looking up from a half-eaten burger.

"You guys are from over the pond, from United Kingdog, aren't you? Oh, I just love your accents. Please, say some words, say something to me – anything!"

"Woof," replied Wag.

After eating at the 'Barking Mad Diner' the next item on their list was to check out a bit more of Washington D.C. Why were the houses so posh-looking and everywhere so damn-dog expensive?

"Let's find a few places to put our pee," suggested Wag.

Scally nodded. "Good idea. We need to mark some territory first, get our scent out there."

"Nothing better than peeing on another dog's doorstep," agreed Wag, cheerily. He was happy at just the thought. And a little later, he was even happier after the action. He had just scraped the ground with his back feet when a large black SUV screeched to a halt beside them. A dog-in-black stepped out.

Not any old dog-in-black. It was the same figure that had been stalking them since they had arrived. Then another dog-in-black stepped out of the car. They were built like military-grade war dogs and looked as tough as a brick doghouse. In fact, they looked identical. It was almost impossible to know one from the other.

"They're a strange breed," whispered Scally under his breath.

"Don't look dog-natural to me," replied Wag in a low voice. They both knew something was up.

The first dog-in-black indicated that they should get into the SUV. Wag and Scally hardly had a moment to let a dastardly thought enter their heads before they were grabbed by both dog-in-blacks and bundled into the back seat of the SUV and driven away at top speed. They were separated from the two dogs sitting up front by a hard glass screen. They could see them but little else. They tried the door handles. Also locked.

"Not getting out until they let us out," said Scally.

"Let's sit back and enjoy the ride then," mumbled Wag as he fumbled with what looked like the door of a small cabinet in front of him. "Don't tell me these huge city tanks don't have a mini bar."

But Scally had turned his attention elsewhere. He was looking out at the passing roads, trying to gain a sense of location. Then he knew exactly where they were heading. The large iconic building loomed up ahead.

CHAPTER THREE

Meeting with the Presidog of Ameridog

The SUV thundered through the back-door gates and came to a sudden halt. The door was opened from the outside and a familiar face appeared.

"Took a while to find you guys. You're the slipperiest lemons I've come across in all my years." It was the Irish wolfhound McMurphy, their airport chauffeur.

Scally brushed down his waistcoat. "Got to check out the smell of a city before making a reservation."

"Yeah, got to get to know some of the ass before you meet with its head," added Wag in a somewhat less elegant way.

McMurphy didn't look like he was on the same page, but it didn't matter. He just shook his head. He knew the boys from the United Kingdog had their own way of doing things. He took them through the security check and then through some winding corridors that seemed to go on forever.

"Who designed this place?" asked Wag loudly, "some baby-wetting poodle with a long-corridor infatuation?"

McMurphey coughed. "Actually, it was designed by a compatriot of mine, an Irish archidog called Hoban."
Wag shrugged. He thought it best not to reply with a witty comeback. You couldn't be sure how far these guy's elastic-humor would stretch.

They came to a posh-looking room with a few sofas and armchairs laid out in an apparently arranged fashion. McMurphy told them to wait, saying the Presidog of the United States of Ameridog would meet them shortly. They were left to themselves. Well, not exactly to themselves. There were the two brick-built dogs-in-black standing silently at either end of the room.

"Maybe we should toss them a bone?" suggested Wag.

"Nah, leave the brutes be. We've got to toss with a bigger bone soon enough," replied Scally as he relaxed into one of the upholstered armchairs.

Wag had half-finished the jar of jellybeans when the door opened and a white poodle with a mop of frizzy hair sauntered into the room with a broad grin. His beaming face looked as if he'd just solved the riddle of the dogiverse – or else had found the perfect door frame to scratch his back against.

"I'm Frumpus, the Presidog of the United States of Ameridog," said the poodle with a self-gloating air. "But you guys already know that. Just call me Frumpus. We're all friends here."

"This is Wag," said Scally pointing over to his buddy who was popping another jellybean into his mouth. "And I'm Scally. We're here on behalf of Dog Intelligence, United Kingdog. But you already know that."

Frumpus laughed. "Ease it down, boys. No standing on ceremony here. I'm a regular kind of dog, even if I do admit I'm certainly not your average poodle."

That made Wag wonder just what an average poodle might be, but he decided not to pursue the thought. Instead, he inspected the poodle's mop of frizzy hair. And he soon concluded that although outwardly frizzy, it was nonetheless in exact position as if each hair had been manicured into place.

'"Mmm…artificially constructed messiness," thought Wag to himself. He made a note to himself to make a mental note of it. And he'd let Scally do the talking, as usual.

"Psst," continued Frumpus. "Come closer. I need to tell you boys a big secret. It's a real biggie, and I've been waiting for you guys like a baseball bat waiting for the pitcher." He beckoned for Wag and Scally to move in closer. Scally gave a cautious look over at the two huge dogs-in-black. "Ah, don't worry about those blockheads. They've been genetically modified to be special ops. They're as tough as a poo-whipping stick but they've got no brains because we brain wiped them too. It's marvelous. Amazing, really. Ameridog mind technology at its finest – none of that foreign cheap technology." Frumpus chuckled to himself. Then he mimed some words with his mouth. Wag and Scally didn't understand a thing. Frumpus tried again to mime the words.

"Sorry, Mister Presidog, but you're going to have to speak," whispered Scally.

"Yeah, dude – like give us some words to play with." Wag just thought it best to add a bit more. Generally, it doesn't hurt.

Frumpus cleared his throat. "We're being *in-va-ded*." The final three syllables were said slowly and with emphasis. "Follow me. We can't talk here." He then nodded over to the dogs-in-black and stamped his poodle paw on the floor. "To the bunker, boys."

They all left the posh salon with its upholstered furniture and followed one of the dogs-in-black as it took them through a series of connecting corridors. The other dog-in-black remained as the rear guard.

Frumpus didn't say a word as the group trotted down one corridor after another; then some steps down; through several mega-thick reinforced steel doors; then more corridors followed by more steps down. It seemed to both Wag and Scally that this was like going down some dubious rabbit hole. It was surely one of those rabbit holes that were so cleverly disguised as a rabbit hole that in fact they were not rabbit holes at all – and at the end there were no rabbits.

Sure enough. They arrived at a thicker-than-thick reinforced steel concrete door that when opened revealed - no rabbits. Wag and Scally curiously stepped inside.

"Ah, it's just another war room," said Wag, peering around. They'd both seen ones like this back in London, such as the one situated underneath Barkingham Palace where Queenie and the Firm lived. The three of them – Frumpus, Wag, and Scally – were alone inside the deep subterranean bunker. Outside, the two dogs-in-black guarded entry. Aside from the communications desk and consoles, there was a large meeting table. Low lights along the walls lit up the bunker. Frumpus sat down and patted his sweating brow. All this exercise and worry had stressed him out. His once immobile mop of frizzy white hair now flopped over his face. He wiped it back with a slick gesture and then sat up in his chair with an attempted air of superiority.

"Yes, boys – we're being invaded. Invaded, I say – *in-va-ded*. And it's those damn commies. The commies are a-coming and this Presidog is gonna be ready for them." He slammed his poodle paw onto the table. "This Presidog is going on a war footing. If it's war they want, then the United States of Ameridog is going to fight them. And I'll make Ameridog great again!"

"Isn't the United States of Ameridog already great?" asked Scally.

Frumpus pouted. "Yeah, but, y'know. Like, even greater, yeah?"

"If we can help you, we will," said Scally, looking all serious. Wag decided it was best not to open his mouth. He knew he'd only say something that wouldn't help the situation. He preferred to let Scally do the talking in this case. "So, tell us what the situation is," continued Scally.
Frumpus babbled away. Between all the *errs* and *yeahs* it worked out that Frumpus was certain that some evil, insidious, dark force was infiltrating his Cabinet and replacing its members. The White House administration was being replaced with spies.

"But it would be obvious if your Cabinet were being replaced with foreign agents, wouldn't it?" asked Scally, not quite sure of the plot.

"Ah, but not so! It's because they still look the same."

"The same?!" said Wag and Scally together.

"Yeah, dudes. That's the most twisted part of it. My Dog Cabinet looks the same, they act the same, they talk the same – the same Secretaries of State, Energy, Education, blah blah blah – but they're…" Frumpus leaned forward and rounded his mouth. "But they're not real dogs – they're clones!"

"Whoa - that's heavy dog-metal. Clones!" Wag shook his head. He couldn't keep silent on that one.

"If that's true," added Scally, "then this is some serious humdinger. How do you know if they're clones if they look, act, and talk the same?"

"Sniff my butt," replied Frumpus.

Scally backed away. "Sorry, I didn't mean to offend."

"No, no – I mean, actually, sniff my butt. Come over here and smell me. Seriously. I want you guys to smell my butt." Wag and Scally both pulled a face. "Oh, don't get all Brit-pompous on me. You're both dogs like the rest of us. Come on, do what a dog does best – sniff my butt!"

Scally looked over at Wag, and Wag looked over at Scally. They were both thinking the same thing – that white poodles always have a brown stain patch at the back. Scally tapped his paws on the table and gave Wag his pondering look. Wag got the message. It was down to the revolutionaries to do the dirty work. It always was and always will be. Not much changes over the generations. Wag got up and strolled over whilst Frumpus got off his chair and dropped on all fours. Wag rubbed his nose a couple of times and then breathed out deeply. With the most cautious of respiratory intakes, he took his first dose of a presidential whiff.

"Yeah, not exactly rosemary but definitely the unmistakable aroma of the anal scent glands. Hasn't been emptied for a while." He sniffed again. "A German origin poodle…or could be French."

Frumpus pulled away and sat down. "German origin. Certainly German. Don't give me that French fries rubbish." Now he did look offended. Wag strolled back and sat down. Job done.

"That's my point," continued Frumpus. "I know the others are clones because their asses don't smell."

"No anal scent sacs," added Scally.

"Precisely!" Frumpus pushed back his frizzy mop. "See, you can't clone the sent sac. These guys are all like the real thing, but they can't smell like the real thing. And it's been happening for a while now. I first noticed it when I was in the bathroom with…" Frumpus suddenly stopped talking. "Boys, forget the details. The commies are getting our great Ameridogs cloned, and we need to stop it!" But first things were first. And Wag and Scally needed to get some first-paw proof.

Soon, they were all back upstairs and sitting in the Oval Office of the White House. One after another, Frumpus called in the secretaries of his Cabinet who he now considered to be clones. Luckily, this was not all the Cabinet. They hadn't yet replaced the Director of National Intelligence, the Secretary of Dogland Security, or the Vice-Presidog. Yet they had certainly gotten to many of the rest. As they were called in, Frumpus would involve them in some policy discussion, or Scally would engage them in diplomat chit-chat, whilst Wag would do the revolutionary respiratory rear-end walk-by.

A few hours later, Wag, Scally, and Frumpus were relaxing in the Presidog's private, private quarters. Frumpus sipped from his glass of diet cola whilst Wag and Scally drank straight out of their bottled beers. Wag had agreed that many of the secretaries of Frumpus's Cabinet had no anal scent glands. They were clones. And that was going to make things difficult. They knew that as soon as they let on that they knew, then the whole ball game would change. It was best to let the other side – whoever they were – to keep on thinking that their clones were safe and that Frumpus had no clue. The Frumpus part would be easier to keep going. Yet how much time did they have before the other side would make their move? What were the objectives of the clones?

Frumpus was sure it was a plot to take over the White House, and then to have control over the United States of Ameridog.

"But the Cold War is over," said Scally, shaking his head. "Are you sure you're not just pointing the paw at the Rushindogs because of your conditioned beliefs?"

Frumpus looked blank. "What's my air conditioning beliefs got to do with anything? It's the Rushindogs because they've always disliked Ameridog. As it was once, so it shall be until the dead dawn of our era."

Scally still couldn't understand why it would be the Rushindogs. Maybe it was some plot by the arch-evil mastermind Pumperknickel. Scally had been wanting something to pin onto Pumperknickel for a long time now. Maybe this was it?

"Pumper…who?" asked Frumpus after listening to Scally's argument.

"Pumperknickel is the most cunning con-dog in the world. He's been conning organizations and governments the world over into conflicts. This is his *modus operandi*."

"I don't care if this Pumperpicklepepper can speak Italian or not. I just know this is that damn Russian Wolfhound Glutin and his Rushindog cohorts," snapped Frumpus. He then flicked a switch on his desk and shouted, "bring in Podenko."

A few moments later, a stocky German Shephard dog strutted into the room and saluted. Wag looked him over casually and swigged from his second bottle of beer. He'd seen plenty of hunting dogs like this German Shephard. They were loyal and well trained. They were also strong brawlers and maulers. Wouldn't be good to get into a fight with them.

"This is Podenko. He's Captain of US Presidog Guards. You can trust him. He's one of my boys. And he's got a damn fine set of anal scent glands too. Would you guys like to take a sniff?" Wag and Scally both held up their paws in lightning speed.

"We trust your word – you're the Presidog," replied Scally, smiling.

Podenko strutted around the room as if marking his territory. He gave off the scent of the kind of guy who looks like he doesn't get to laughing a great deal. "Right," said Podenko, clearing his throat, "we need to get perspective here. It's possible we have some Rushindog intervention on our turf. What I'm going to tell you here in this room is top secret confidential. It stays in this room."

Wag raised his hand. "Does that mean when we leave this room, we have to forget what you just told us? Because if not, then the information can't stay in this room, it has to travel with us." Podenko looked over at Frumpus who just shrugged.

"Well," resumed the Captain of US Presidog Guards, "let us agree to agree not to share this information and keep it in our heads." Wag nodded in agreement. That seemed fair to him. Podenko walked over to a console and pushed some buttons.

A familiar figure appeared on the large wall screen.

"This is our Number One suspect – Glutin, the de facto Head of Rushindog."

The image showed a Borzoi, Russian Wolfhound breed. He was muscular, bare-chested, and dressed in commando pants. Podenko pressed a button and another picture flicked into view. This time it showed Glutin in white martial arts clothes doing a *I'm-gonna-chop-you* pose. It wasn't very convincing. Another picture came on, this time showing the Russian Wolfhound leaning back on a bed of fur and licking his own paws.

"Looks very cat-like," said Scally, tilting his head.

"Glutin has deceptive feminine qualities – a bit like myself," added Frumpus.

"Isn't Glutin known to be narcissistic also?" asked Wag.

"The point is," interrupted Podenko, slightly irritated, "that we have to know for sure if Glutin is responsible for the White House clone invasion. We've already had several cyber-attacks and email hacking from them. We know the Rushindogs are good at this type of tech thing."

"Yet it's a long way from cyber-attack to cloning," added Scally, still unconvinced.

Podenko gave a hard, stony look. "Gentlemen, we've gone from the Cold War to the Clone Wars. Either way, we're at war."

A short time later and they were all back in the deep underground bunker again. The underground bunker became an operative war room, and a plan was hatched. It wasn't a particularly good plan either. It was more like – 'hey, you nice guys from United Kingdog, go and find out what's happening. Start with the Rushindog connection first.' Podenko put down a file on local Rushindog connections and left after giving everyone a serious eye-to-eye look. Frumpus was looking pleased with himself.

"Hey, guys, want to hear a truly fantastic joke? It's fantastic because I came up with it, and I come up with the best jokes – just ask my ex-wives. Here goes: what does a dyslexic dog believe in?" Wag and Scally wisely remained silent. They knew this was not going to end well. "A dyslexic dog believes in the great God in the sky!" Frumpus burst out laughing and gurgled from his diet cola. "Get it? God is dog backwards. A dyslexic dog makes the Great Dog into God – hah!"
Wag and Scally hid their shame behind unflinching faces. They had been well-trained for times such as this when restraint and fortitude are required.

Soon, but not soon enough, they were back in their chauffeur-driven car with McMurphy behind the wheel.

"Where to, guys?"

"Take us to 'The Barking Mad Diner,'" replied Wag.

A short time later, the same golden Labrador waitress from before came over to take their order. When she saw who it was, she broke out into a huge smile.

"Oh, it's my new favorites from United Kingdog. I just love you guys already." Wag smiled and ordered a double chili burger with extra chilies and a double splash of tabasco sauce. Scally ordered a turkey burger with Dijon mustard. The waitress frowned. "Sorry sir, we don't have day-john mustard. Would you like Ameridog mustard?"

"That's my girl," said Wag with a grin. "What's your name, sweetie?"

"My name's Tuesday. What's yours?"

"I'm Wag, and he's Scally."

"Tuesday Adams. My full name is Tuesday Adams."

"I'm just Wag and he's just Scally. You can call me Wag and him, you can call him Scally."

"You can call me Tuesday."

"I hope I can call you any day. As they say, a Tuesday by any other name is still a day of the week. That's a line by the famous United Kingdog poet Dogspeare, by the way."

"It's beautiful. It's so deep."

"Yeah – it's dog deep. Remember I said it

first, my Tuesday." As the waitress trotted away with a new shine, Wag turned to his buddy. "Judas Dogpriest, Scally. I think I've just got a new favorite day of the week."

"I always thought you preferred Sundays. Fine, Wag. But let's save Ameridog from the clone invasion first. I don't want a war on my watch."

Wag shrugged. "Sure. It's the Rushindogs first – golden Labradors later. Where do we start?" Wag was looking forward to his double chili burger with extra chilies.

CHAPTER FOUR

Hanging Out with the Rushindogs

They looked across the street at the entrance to the fruit and vegetable market. It appeared clean and legit from the outside, yet they knew dark dealings were going on behind the façade. It was time to investigate and infiltrate. And, if necessary, buy and eat some fruit along the way.

Wag and Scally shuffled across the busy street in their undercover mode. Both were wearing casual worker's clothes, looking a bit scuffed and ruffled. Wag wore his favorite tatty beret which he saved for covert operations. They entered the bustling market and immediately were hit by the din and commotion of buyers and sellers shouting and haggling. Scally sniffed. He smelt the odor of ambiguity. Wag sniffed. He smelt the odor of intrigue, dried pee, and rotten vegetables. Together it made for a telling mix. According to the top-secret file that Podenko had let them see, this market was operated by the Rushindog mafia as an import/export venue. And it wasn't only fruit and veg they were dealing with. Wag and Scally needed to get closer to the operation to find out if there were any connections. It was alleged that the Dogfather of Rushindog mafia here in Washington, a certain Don Ivansky, had close ties with Glutin. If there was a cloning conspiracy going on, then Don Ivansky was certain to know about it – possibly even be in on it. The last thing Frumpus needed right now was a CloneGate Conspiracy to erupt in the media. The elections were less than a year away, and Frumpus was desperate to hold onto power. *Make Ameridog Bark Again* was his slogan – but you cannot *MABA* when you have an invasion of clones without the proper anal scent sacs. It was a huge dilemma, perhaps the biggest in Ameridog's history, and Frumpus knew this only too well.

Wag and Scally made their reconnaissance. On the surface, everything seemed like a normal madcap market. But behind it all there was a network of dirty money and dog-bad crime. Illegal money was moving from paw to paw in a place like this. But Wag and Scally were not here for the crime or dirty money. They needed information. Now it was time to enact their plan.

"You ready, Wag?" asked Scally with a cautious smile.

Wag nodded. "Let's show them some Britdog style." Wag grabbed a zucchini off from a nearby stall and began hitting Scally over the head with it. "You dirty underwear sniffer!"

"Suffocate in my nose hair!" shouted back Scally as he grabbed a red pepper and hurled it at Wag's head. Then he jumped onto Wag and started to pound his rump.

"Son of a walrus," roared Wag as he swung around trying to push Scally off from him. The insults continued – *...you oven licker! ...you horse-hair scrubber! ...you lousy lice breeder! ...you sea-chef assistant!* ...on and on until the market vendors were screaming for calm – and to get their stolen vegetables back. The dog scuffle and the insults continued until two pairs of heavy paws pulled Wag and Scally apart and dragged them off. The vendors all cheered together, delighted to be rid of the vegetable throwers.

Wag and Scally were dragged and then shaken like seed sacks until dumped on the floor. They were in a back warehouse. Although not sure exactly where they were, they both knew it was where they were meant to be. Two large Caucasian Shepherd Dogs stood over them, one looking mean and the other looking double-mean.

"Ah, I see you've met Yeltsky and Borsky," said a voice. An intelligent face scrutinized the two newcomers who had been dragged from the market for causing a ruckus. "I don't care for such unruly commotion on my turf," said the boss dog. "It's rather uncouth and shows a lack of discipline. Yeltsky, did you find any identification?"

Yeltsky proudly handed the two ID cards to his boss, Don Ivansky. Scally smiled inwardly, knowing how he had left their IDs in easy to find pockets – and now this Yeltsky, a not-so-clever Caucasian Shepherd, was feeling proud. But Don Ivansky was an altogether different breed. Scally looked him over discreetly. He was a West Siberian Laika, a breed known for their alertness and vigilance. Don Ivansky had a face that puffed with experience. It was a face that had seen a lot of action and knew a lot about cutting corners. And cutting off paws.

Don Ivansky pawed over the two IDs. "So, we have Rushindog ancestry here. Wagorsky and Scallovsky. Where's your homeland, boys?"

"Our families are originally from Vladi-dogstok, in Dogberia," replied Scally. "We're second generation in Ameridog. But our blood is in Dogberia."

Don Ivansky peered closer at the new intruders. "Mmm. Well, you Wagorsky, you certainly have some Mongol blood in you. I can see it in your face."

"Vladidogstock sits on the border of the Asian territories," replied Wag. "My father came over from the steppes. But my blood is Rushindog."

"And why the fighting in my market?"

Wag shrugged. "We get to scuffling sometimes when things get desperate. We're in hard times."

"We didn't know it was your market," added Scally.

Don Ivansky stepped closer to them both and sniffed. "You guys smell odd. Does one of you wear old perfume?" Wag flashed a quick glance over at Scally.

"Never mind," said Don Ivansky. "We could use some extra paws around here. You boys open for some hard work."

"Yes Sir!" replied Wag and Scally in unison.

A little later, Wag and Scally – or Wagorsky and Scallovsky as they were now known – were in a rear warehouse packing crates onto trucks. They were the new hired paws. And now that they were inside, they could take a sniff around at the operation. Don Ivansky was running the main import-export business for this side of the US. Wag and Scally needed to know, double dog-quick time, whether any clones were coming in.

"They're certainly not going to be coming in

disguised as vegetables," stated Wag in a sarcastic tone.

Scally shook his head. He had to agree with Wag on that one. Something just didn't smell right about the Rushindog connection. Why would Glutin risk an all-out war by putting clones in the Ameridog government? If he got found out, the stakes would be too high. And the clones have been recognized. If there's any whiff of Glutin involvement, then it's a declaration of an international dogfight. Too risky. But still, they had to check it out.

Next morning, Wag and Scally were at the larger central Washington warehouse waiting for a shipment to come in. As a cover, they had rented a dingy apartment near to the marketplace where many emigrants were living. They had to fit in as best they could. It also meant not washing for a while. And, for Scally, it meant not using his preferred dog shampoo. Sacrifices had to be made. Wag chewed on his Tutti-Frutti gum and spat on the ground as he adjusted his tattered beret. Wag was in his element. Scally pulled up his oversized pants and leant against a steel column with a toothpick in his mouth. The shipment was being transferred by truck from the inbound ship *Beelzebub's Grandson*. Four truckloads of crates were expected any minute. Other heavy-duty dudes were hanging around the warehouse too. They both suspected that they were being watched, as the new guys, so they couldn't be seen acting out of sorts or any funny business.

The metal doors rolled up and the convoy of trucks rolled in. Yeltsky and Borsky took charge and ordered the transfer of the crates. They called Wagorsky and Scallovsky over and with the others they began shifting the stock. Some of the crates were sealed shut whilst others were open. The open ones looked to be full of fruits and vegetables. As they lifted these open crates both Wag and Scally stealthily slipped their paws in to feel down below. It was fruits and vegetables all the way down. But the sealed crates? They couldn't get inside them for now. When all the crates had been loaded onto the trucks, they jumped into the back and rolled off to the market warehouse. The open crates were off-loaded but the closed crates remained on the trucks.

"Hey, new guys, come with me to the next drop-off," shouted Yeltsky, the gruff Caucasian Shepherd.

Two of the trucks continued to the next location. Half an hour later and they arrived at another warehouse; a smaller one with only a few high windows. They entered and stacked the closed crates at one end.

"We need two volunteers to take night duty here. Any volunteers?" There were only four of them - Yeltsky, Wag, Scally, and one other. No one volunteered. "Good. Then Wagorsky and Scallovsky, you take the shift. It's agreed," said Yeltsky. Then he and the other guy drove off with the two trucks.

The warehouse was dimly lit. At one end sat the new crates, whilst at the other was a couple of old sofas, a table, and a small sink with shelf and a mini fridge. An old kettle stood there with a few ceramic mugs and a tin of teabags.

"It's like being at home," commented Wag as he picked up the tin of teabags. He sniffed. "Smells like DG Tips."

"Smells like something," replied Scally, uncertain of events. He paced around the floor whilst Wag brewed two mugs of tea. They had gotten into the Rushindog organization, yet now they needed to get their paws onto some decent intel. Scally was still not convinced that the White House cloning operation was a Rushindog tactic – far too risky, he kept repeating to himself. Cyber-hacking was more the Rushindog style. The cloning was technically sophisticated, and yet the practicalities appeared too invasive and lacked subtlety. The whole thing smelled more like revenge, anger, or even desperation. Scally was convinced that someone, somewhere, wanted to hurt Frumpus, and to inflict damage upon him as Presidog. It seemed more like a personal vendetta.

Scally took the mug of tea from Wag and

continued to pace up and down in deep thought. Wag watched his partner, knowing very well his tactics and moods. He knew his friend Scally was trying to get his mind into the deeper intricacies of the mission. Wag strolled around the warehouse, brushing away a large fly that buzzed too close to his head. He arrived at the crates and gave them a tap. There's no fruits or vegetables in here, he thought to himself. He walked back to Scally.

"There's only one thing we can do whilst we're here for the night" said Wag. Scally nodded. He knew it too.

Several minutes later and they had managed to pry open one of the lids of a crate. On first inspection it looked to be filled with straw. Wag stuck in his paw and felt around.

"Got something," he said. He brought out his hand and they both stared at what they had discovered. Expensive chocolate. "Real chocolate or cloned chocolate?" Wag grinned.

"Why don't you sniff the back end of it," replied Scally sarcastically.

They opened up another crate. And then another. All of them contained bars of expensively wrapped chocolate. It was not what they were hoping to find. Not that they were expecting to find clones, yet at least it could have been some clues that might help them to understand what was going on. A trade in chemicals, or laboratory equipment, or something else of the sort. But no, it was a smuggled delivery of expensive chocolate bars for spoilt, upper crust aristodogs.

"Better get the lids put back on," said Scally with a sigh. A whole night wasted. And now they had to wait it out until dawn, with only mugs of DG Tips to see them through. It was going to be a long night.

And long it was. It seemed like several dog days before the dawn finally arose and shone its early light into the dim warehouse. Morning shadows crept along the floor. Wag drowsily pulled himself up from the sofa and again brushed away the annoying fly. Chocolate, flies, and boredom, he thought. Is this really the way to serve the United Kingdog?

After two more mugs of tea, the warehouse door was unlocked and in stepped Yeltsky and Borsky with huge dog-smug grins.

"Hello boys," greeted Yeltsky in a gruff voice.

"Come on, we want to show you something," said Borsky, pointing over to the crates. The four of them trotted over to where the crates were stacked. "What do you think are in these?" asked Borsky. Wag shrugged and feigned disinterest.

"Waxed fruits and plastic-wrapped vegetables?" suggested Scally. Yeltsky and Borsky laughed. And then they kept on laughing until the joke had worn so thin it had faded into air. Hearing some noise, Wag and Scally turned around to see a bunch of Rushindog heavies move in on them. There was no time to struggle. The next thing they knew, they were tied with heavy ropes and strapped to two chairs.

"What the dog-arse smellbrain is this?" shouted Wag as he struggled against his tightly knotted ropes.

"Let it play out, Wag – let it play out," whispered Scally to his buddy. He suspected that sooner or later something like this had to happen to get them closer to the center of what was going on. If you can't get to where you need to go by stealth, then let the other side bring you in directly – that was Scally's reasoning.

A few moments later and Don Ivansky entered the warehouse. The West Siberian Laika looked cool and confident. He strutted up to Wag and Scally and peered at them calmly.

"Chocolate," he said. "That's what we have in the boxes – expensive imported chocolate. We smuggle it in, so we don't have to pay taxes. If the Presidog doesn't have to pay taxes, why should we? Then again, you knew it was chocolate anyway. So, let's not argue about it." Don Ivansky turned to his heavies. "Okay, get these crates out of here. I need this place empty faster than a date with diarrhea." The rough henchmen jumped into action and started to haul the crates out.

"We're not arguing. We're only wondering," replied Scally with an equal calm.
Don Ivansky pulled out a phone-sized device from his pocket and unfolded it. It looked somewhat like a portable games console. He swiveled some screen buttons and the large buzzing fly circled around Wag and Scally's heads.

"A drone," said Scally with a nod. "Impressive."

"Yes, isn't it?"agreed Don Ivansky. "Rushindog made. It's amazing how small these drones can get. Just think of it, what would happen if you got a fly in the White House. Would it be just an ordinary fly buzzing around?"

"I've always disliked flies – now I hate them," grumbled Wag.

"They have their uses. In this day and age, we don't need brute force. We find that stealth works much better."

"And stealth is what the Rushindogs are best at," said Scally.

"Exactly," replied Don Ivansky. He looked again at his monitor. "Ah, and here is the video feed. Two boys cracking open the lids of my crates. And disappointment at finding chocolate. Either way, you've committed a crime on my turf." Don Ivansky turned to the remaining henchmen. "You can leave us alone now, boys – we're gonna have a little fun."

"I wouldn't call opening smuggled boxes a crime," added Scally.

"True. So true. That's not a crime. The crime is breaking our circle of trust. Within our band of dog-brothers we have a bond of trust. You see, we Rushindogs trust in our circle." Don Ivansky held up his paw and made a circle in the air. "I brought you both into my circle of trust, and you guys just broke it. So now, in return, we're going to break you."

"Wait," called out Wag. "I have something very important to show you."

"What's that?"

"I have a code sign for you. Let me show you the code that I was told to give you. But first you need to untie one paw – just one paw. I can't escape with just one paw now, come on!"

Don Ivansky shrugged. He nodded over to Borsky, who stepped forward and untied some of the rope for Wag to release one paw. "Okay, wise guy. But don't mess around with me or I'll horseradish you."

Wag looked puzzled. "Just come closer so that I can show you the sign…the s-i-g-n." Again, Don Ivansky nodded to Borsky who stepped in close to Wag. Wag held out his paw and moved it in a horizontal figure of eight.

"This is my bond of eternity. Those who are trusted to enter into this bond of eternity are given great secrets."

Borsky was intrigued. He stepped even closer. "Yeah? Such as?"

"Such as a Wagamuffin slap." Saying that, Wag let out a huge swing and punched Borsky square on his nose. Borsky jumped back in shock and then retaliated with a kick toward Wag. Yet Wag was expecting this and had already tilted back his chair. Instead of hitting Wag, Borsky hit the frame of the chair and sent it flying back.

"Take that, you son of a horse behind!" Yet Wag was not lying still. He had a plan in mind, although it involved a bit of pain. Wag had hit his shoulder on the floor, and with the impact he jerked it and crack…his shoulder became floppy. He then wriggled out of his ropes and quickly kicked the chair at the astonished Borsky, making him tumble back. Wag grabbed his shoulder and with a big squeeze he pushed it into place. Just in time. Yeltsky was now lurching forward. With nothing else at hand, Wag grabbed Scally's chair, with Scally still in it, and swung it to bash Yeltsky over the head. Yeltsky dropped down moaning. Wag leapt at Don Ivansky with his trusty tazer in paw and jammed him with it. Don Ivansky also dropped down moaning.

"Fine one, Wag. Yet before you get onto round two of tazing, would you be kind enough to untie me."

"Sure thing, Scally mate."

Wag and Scally were now in charge of the floor. Borsky, Yeltsky, and Don Ivansky were all tied up. They looked dazed from the second bout of tazing. Scally, with his waistcoat now brushed down, was eyeing his opponents.

"Some things should be, and other things shouldn't be. And in the middle, there is an indistinct zone that's grey and muffled. You get me?"

Don Ivansky moaned and shook his head. "No, not really."

"Good," replied Scally, looking content. "I don't like it when I get challenged by a linguistically lesser opponent." Scally took a card out of his waistcoat and, showing it to Don Ivansky, said, "Ring Don Colombo and tell him who's here. Arrange our meeting and we won't need to take matters any further here. We're not at odds with you. You may be criminals, but so are most of the politicians in this world. We've got bigger dogs to fry."

Don Ivansky managed a defiant snarl, whilst Borsky and Yeltsky just sat there drooling.

In the dog underworld, it's not always about dog-eat-dog. That would be a strange, and quite frankly,

an inexcusable form of cannibalism anyway. No. It is
more about making the right connections.

CHAPTER FIVE

The Dogfather Connection

Scally cocked an eye over at Wag. "That was a smart move you pulled back there. What did you do, dislocate your shoulder?"

Wag sniffed, trying to deflect the compliment. "Yeah, well, I saw it done as a trick in the movie *Lethal Dog Gun*. I've been practicing it over the years. It was one hell of a painful journey, but it comes in useful. I wouldn't want to try it too often though." Wag looked over at Borsky and Yeltsky who were still tied up and looking a sorry pair. Don Ivansky was on his phone making some calls. Soon, they hoped, they would be moving from one Dogfather to another.

"Hey!" Scally called over to Don Ivansky after he had finished speaking. "So, what's the score between Glutin and Frumpus anyway? Are you guys trying to start a war?"

Don Ivansky pulled a surprised face. "Don't believe anything you hear and disbelieve twice as much as what you see on the mainstream media. Glutin is actually a fan of Frumpus. He much prefers him over his old rival Distillary Rodbottom. She's a much more dangerous brute."

"Distillary, eh?" That got Scally thinking.

"We Rushindogs don't have anything against Frumpus. Oh, he's a poodle for sure. But poodles are poodles – at least you know what you get with that breed. Glutin gets along with Frumpus. But Distillary. Now she's a different breed altogether. That one's an Ameridog Pit Bull Terrier. You gotta watch out for those."

Don Ivansky was as good as his word. The handover to Don Columdog was arranged. As they parted, Don Ivansky held up his paw in warning.

"Stay schtum about the chocolates. Breathe a word of it and me and you will be having a few words ourselves."

"Don't worry, Don," replied Scally, "on this matter, we won't be breaking your circle of trust." Wag held up his paw to make his eternity symbol.

"Whooh," interrupted Don Ivansky, "you can keep your wagamuffin malarky to yourself."

Like all good first meetings, it was over food in a restaurant. Wag and Scally were dropped off at Luigi

& Dante's Italian restaurant. Inside, it was dimly lit and looked more like someone's basement. They found Don Columdog seated in a private booth eating a plate of spaghetti and clams. Hovering by the table was his bodyguard, and the Great Dane that they had met previously in the alleyway.

"Ah, I see that you both have met Chester before. You gave him quite a tazing. And that gets you an invitation to me. At first, I was going to fry you boys and hang your tails from the overhead cables. Now that you've rustled the fur of those Rushindogs, I might just give you a hearing. Sit down, guys." Don Columdog cut an impressive figure. A well-toned, dark-skinned Rottweiler with sharp, observing eyes. When he looked at you, you knew you were being looked at.

"I'm glad you received my card," said Scally coolly as both he and Wag took a seat across from the local Dogfather. "Nice décor in this place. It has kept its charm."

Wag pointed his paw at the Great Dane. "And no hard feelings, Chester matey – it's just that you jumped us without warning." Chester the Great Dane sniffed but didn't reply. It seemed that he was still licking the wounds of his pride.

"You both are brave boys coming here," continued Don Columdog. "You come over from Britdog and start to mess with the local Dogfathers. You either have a death wish or an incredible desire to find something out. So, what is it that you're looking for, boys - and why should I help you out?"

"It's like this," began Scally, yet he was quickly interrupted by Wag.

"We don't say a thing until we get a decent pizza. I'll have a family sized peperone with extra chilies and a dash of tabasco sauce. Oh, and put a basil leaf on the top. Scally?"

"A four-cheese regular pizza for me. Wag is correct. Food before negotiations."

Don Columdog was a straight-faced, hard-looking fellow yet he seemed firm and fair. Scally had a feeling that despite his criminal dealings he was a patriot at heart, and so decided to edge his bets by disclosing a small part of their relationship with Frumpus. After all, if the Don was a patriot, then this might put them in a good position.

"So, Don Columdog, are you wishing to make Ameridog bark again?" asked Scally finally, after they had finished eating and Scally had just revealed their 'friendship' with Frumpus.

Don Columdog sipped his strong, black Ameridog coffee. "I sure don't want to see this country of ours go barking mad. At the end of the day, I'm with Frumpus. For all his faults, and that poodle has quite a few, he's always been on our side. At least he knows which side to chew his bone. We've had dealings with him in the past too."

"Really?" Scally's interest was pricked.

"Deal us the dirt, Don," added Wag.

Don Columdog pulled on his thick, fat cigar. "Nothing to be dealing you guys. Only to say that our family had dealings with him in New York way back when. We were in the concrete business, and he was in the building business. Naturally, they make a good mix."

"Concrete mixes well," said Wag, offering a pseudo-thought.

"Money mixes better," added Don Columdog. "You know, politics and money are bedfellows. That's why our world has good connections with theirs. We get a sense of what's going on too. We know this country of ours is being infiltrated. And we're gonna do our darned best to make sure that don't happen. Any Presidog that stands up for this country, well, let's just say that we have their back. I want to show you something that may surprise you. Let's go for a ride." Don Columdog stood up and put out his cigar on the plate. His body was a strong build and would be a hard match for any dog fight. Wag considered it a dark day if they were ever to come head-to-head.

Back outside of Luigi & Dante's Italian restaurant the glare of the sunlight was blinding. They waited for Chester to bring over the large black sedan. Wag sat up front with Chester while Scally took a back seat with Don Columdog. The Dogfather lit another fat cigar and the smoke filled the sedan. Scally started to cough.

"Ah, sorry," said Don Columdog with a grin, "I mistook your waistcoat for a smoking jacket."

"It's okay, I guess it's hard to recognize style in Ameridog," replied Scally.

"Touché," called back Wag from the front. The large black sedan criss-crossed the streets and large avenues of Washington D.C. Once again, Wag and Scally got to see just how sprawling the city was. Don Columdog was reeling off his favorite baseball heroes as they drove. Wag and Scally listened only with half-interest. For them, baseball was a reminder of the bygone days of dog slavery when their old masters used to throw balls and expect the dog slaves to return them. Baseball was no different, only that you ran in circles.

After what seemed like far too long, and far too much baseball dribble, the black sedan pulled up beside a building. The sign outside read **Strategic Foresight Consulting**.

The Dogfather needs some consulting? wondered Scally to himself. Yet Wag thought differently. He knew that any company with a trite name like that had to be dealing with other things. Banality was often just a cover story. And too much banality in Ameridog meant that there were too many cover stories covering up the truth. Wag remembered a saying from one of his favorite philosophers, the wise Lo-Poo – *Know that you don't know what you don't know, and don't pretend otherwise.*

Inside, the new smart building was wired up with the latest sensors and tech equipment. Don Columdog led Wag and Scally through a series of full body scans, including the latest paw print scanner. Apparently, they were told by the security guard that the paw scanner can detect each one's unique vein imprint under the surface of the paw skin.

Wag was unimpressed. "They think they can know me from my veins? Superficial, skin-deep technology…it's barking mad," he huffed.

"We live in a tech world now," replied Scally. The three of them entered a clean, almost too clean, room with soft sofas, and were told to wait. The whole place was so organized, efficient, and…there was something else.

Scally spotted it almost immediately. "This whole place appears very sterile. Not the kind of place where you'd have a busy consulting agency. In fact, there's almost no one around. This isn't one of your places, is it?" Scally turned to Don Columdog.

"You're right. I'm passing you over to the Agency. We're all connected. It's no secret that the underdog world has been paw in paw with the Agency for quite some time. Like I said, we're all patriots. You can't sneeze in Washington without getting someone's dribble on your face."

"Sounds like a pub I know back home," said Wag.

The door quietly slid back, and a well-dressed female stepped inside. Wag's jaw suddenly dropped open.

"See, I told you," remarked Don Columdog, "look who's dribbling now."

"Tuesday?" Wag looked astonished. "I think my favorite day of the week has just walked in."

"Nearly, but not quite. Tuesday is my twin sister. I am Thursday. Thursday Adams." Thursday looked exactly like Tuesday except that she wore a pair of spectacles on her nose. It made her look serious and studious. Suddenly, Scally was impressed. Thursday was an elegant Golden Labrador, the same as her twin sister. "Thank you, Don Columdog. We'll be taking the matter from here."

Don Columdog stood up. "Good knowing you, boys. And I wish you success. And if you ever need any cheap cigarettes or a room in Las Vegas, just let me know." Then he turned and left. Wag and Scally turned to Thursday.

"So, you're the Agency?" asked Scally, straightening down his waistcoat.

"And your twin sister is a waitress at the *Barking Mad Diner*?" asked Wag, a little confused.

Thursday smiled as if to herself. "Follow me. I'll explain as we go."

They left the room and walked down several corridors before they arrived at a guarded elevator door. Thursday scanned her paw and the metallic doors opened. The three of them stepped inside. After punching in a code number, the elevator softly began to move down.

"Yes, we're the Agency. Formally called the CIA – the Canine Intelligence Agency."

Scally nodded. His suspicions were right.

"Yes, our agency DI - Dog Intelligence – have dealt with you in the past. Yet I've never heard of a Thursday Adams working here."

"I'm on a need-to-know basis," replied Thursday.

"And we need to know you now?" Scally raised an inquisitive eyebrow.

"Yes, you do, Scally. The both of you do. This is serious business."

"And Tuesday? Why are you CIA and she's a..." Wag seemed a little lost for words. "Well, I mean, just a waitress in a diner?"

Thursday gave Wag a long, hard look. "Looks like she fooled you then. She's good at that, is Tuesday. She's got the charm for it. She's not 'just a waitress.' She's CIA too. She works undercover. She's got contacts on the street. And she's got your number, buster."

Scally laughed.

Wag slapped his paws together. "Dog damn. My favorite day of the week just got brighter." The elevator continued going down. And down. They both thought it was going a long way down.

"Strategic Foresight Consulting isn't a mining company, is it?" asked Scally. Yet his irony was lost on Thursday. Scally didn't care though. A Thursday by any other name is still a day of the week, as the poet Dogspeare would say.

The doors finally opened. Now the place was busy. They were deep underground in a CIA secret operation base. Staff were busy walking between offices, all looking super serious with concentrated looks on their faces. Wag thought that perhaps they all needed to eat a bit more fruit. It would loosen their bowels a bit. But maybe the Canine Intelligence Agency were not particularly into loose bowels. Perhaps they preferred tart faces. Either way, faces don't make an agency any more than paw prints make a dog's body. Wag was once again reminded of his favorite philosopher, the wise Lo-Poo, who said: *Don't think yourself wise if you first can't escape from your own sense of cleverness*. Lo-Poo was wise indeed – Wag was sure of that.

Thursday led them into a large empty room that had a darkened window across the full length of one of the walls.

"Take a seat," she instructed them. Thursday pressed a button, and the dark window became transparent. Through the glass, Wag and Scally could see what appeared to be a large laboratory with various lab-coated staff working on…

"What?!"

Both Wag and Scally leaned forward to get a better look. What they saw was a room full of immobile dogs, of various breeds and types. They stood erect, without moving, as if robots.

Scally clucked his tongue, something which he ordinarily does not do. "These are clones."

Thursday nodded. Her spectacles fell slightly down her nose. She slowly nudged them back up. Scally noted that. He liked the gesture.

"But these are not the clones you're looking for," said Wag with a strange move of his paw.

"What?"

"Sorry," interrupted Scally, "Wag's seen too many films. So, who's running this operation here?"

"I am," replied Thursday, looking straight at Scally. "I'm the Head of Operations here." Scally's terrier nose twitched. He suddenly realized he may have a new favorite day of the week that was far more than just a name.

"Excellent. That's pure."

Wag coughed into his paw. "Ahem, I think we may need some filling in here."

Thursday nodded. "First, I need to get you guy's top-level Q clearance."

The United States of Ameridog had always kept a 'special relationship' with the United Kingdog. This was the only way that Wag and Scally could be granted top secret Q-level privileges. Wag and Scally listened carefully as Thursday explained to them the secret CIA cloning program. It had initially been developed as a back-up security plan for their top-level politicians. Those in the top positions, such as the Presidog and the Vice-Presidog, would have clones made of them as a security replacement. In the older days, they would each have a lookalike substitute who could fill in for them on some occasions where security could not be guaranteed, or where there were suspicions. Yet since the day of the 35th Presidog's assassination, it became extremely difficult to find willing lookalike substitutes.

"What do you mean, exactly?" asked Scally.

"Well. Johndog Kennedy wasn't killed on November 22nd 1963, in Texas – not technically, anyway. His lookalike substitute was assassinated. There were doubts about that day, so Johndog had his substitute to fill in. After the killing, substitute applications all dried up. So, we had to switch to an alternative plan."

"Which was to create clones as substitutes," added Scally.

"Precisely. And since…"

"Whoa, hold on," interrupted Wag. "So, what happened to Johndog Kennedy, the real Johndog?"

Thursday paused, as if thinking it over. "Well, since you both now have Q clearance, then technically I can tell you. Of course, the real Johndog Kennedy had to retreat from the public eye. He could never be seen in public again or our substitute program would be uncovered."

"What did he do – grow a long beard and become a recluse?" asked Wag with genuine interest.

"Not exactly. He went into a top-secret military protection program. And then, erh…" Thursday seemed to hesitate.

"Yes? And, erh what?" insisted Wag.

"Then his top-secret military program, or unit, went rogue."

"Went rogue?!"

"Yes. They broke away and, allegedly, formed their own autonomous protection unit that, we believe, calls itself QA."

Scally's ears pricked up. He recalled reading a brief memo on QA in the top-secret file that *W* had given them before leaving on the mission. Scally delved into his memory. Yes, that was it. "If I'm correct, then QA is a highly secretive organization that is sworn to protect every legitimate Presidog. It is alleged to be made up from the highest military personnel as well as high-ranking politicians and other 'dogs of influence.' It has given itself the mandate to protect the true sovereignty of the United States of Ameridog."

Thursday looked impressed. There was more to this Scally than she had first given credit for. "So, you've heard of them?"

Both Wag and Scally nodded, as if wisely.

"We at the CIA have been trying to track them for years. But they've got the very best military intelligence protecting them. They're more elusive than an invisible sidewalk."

"Or, as we would say in the United Kingdog," said Scally, "they're more elusive than an invisible pavement." He smiled. Thursday smiled back and pushed the spectacles back up her nose.

"And what about them over there?" asked Wag, pointing to several strong looking dog-clones.

"Ah yes. They haven't been dressed yet. We'll get some dark clothes onto them. They're the Presidog's personal bodyguards."

"The dogs-in-black?" Scally looked over at the muscular breeds.

"Exactly. The CIA clones them the most. They always go into active service, whereas the others are substitutes that may, or may not, go into service."

"Are all the Presidog's bodyguards these clones?"

"Yes. All of them."

Scally looked over at Wag. He sensed

something suspicious. "So, why are you telling us all this?"

Thursday looked serious. "We know about the cloning 'situation' in the White House."

"You do?" Scally thought for a second. "But Frumpus doesn't know that you know, right?"

"That's right. There's not much that goes on in Washington D.C. that the CIA doesn't know about. We practically run the place."

You mean you practically own the place, thought Wag.

"And so, if the CIA knows there's clones in the Presidog's Cabinet, then why haven't you acted on it yet?" asked Scally.

Thursday subtly rolled her eyes around the room. She paused. Scally noted the pause. "Well," she continued, "the CIA cannot make any move until we are sure about the situation and who may be behind it. We're currently monitoring the situation."

"Monitoring the situation?" echoed Wag. "What, like sitting back in armchairs and watching your favorite series on Petflix until a solution comes along?"

"Something like that." This time, Thursday really did roll her eyes. Then she cleared her throat. "I'm glad that you've both enjoyed our facilities. It was our pleasure, as the CIA, to be honest and transparent with you, our friends over in the United Kingdog. If there's any help you need from us, just let us know. Well then, I think we're all done here. Let's leave, shall we?"

Wag and Scally followed Thursday back to the elevator. It seemed as if all the other staff members around the place were deliberately ignoring them. Perhaps, thought Scally, everyone kept out of the boss's way.

As the elevator was rising, Scally continued to analyze the situation. Why had they been shown the cloning laboratory? Were they supposed to learn something from this? What was Thursday trying to tell them by not telling them? Things were not adding up. He turned to look at Thursday. Scally's sensitive terrier nose was sniffing to pick up a scent of instinct. There – he noticed it. The very slightest of twitches in Thursday's nose. She too was indicating something. But not here. They couldn't speak here. He knew that. Scally looked over at Wag, and he then rubbed his nose in a certain way that only Wag knew. He understood immediately. Just in time. The elevator door opened, and they were back into the pristine environment of the Strategic Foresight Consulting offices. A guard approached to escort them both out.

Scally licked his lips. "I'm feeling a little peckish. I could do with getting a bite to eat soon. What about you, Wag, old fellow?"

Wag rubbed his stomach. "I reckon I could eat a stranded walrus."

"Why don't we pop on over to your favorite diner, get ourselves some decent Ameridog food?"

"Ey, a great idea, Scally. Sounds like a plan to me." Wag and Scally said their formal, polite goodbyes to Thursday and thanked her for showing them around. They left the building and hailed a taxi.

As soon as a taxi pulled up, Wag and Scally jumped into the back seat.

"Where to, gov?" asked the driver.

"Follow that car!" shouted Wag.

"What car?"

Wag shrugged. "I don't know, any car! I just always wanted to say that in a US taxi."

The taxi driver sighed. "Yeah, you buddy and a thousand others too. Save that baloney for New York. This is Washington. Get serious or get out."

"To the *Barking Mad Diner*," said Scally. The taxi pulled away.

CHAPTER SIX

A Mad, Mad Day with the CIA

Scally was feeling uneasy. He had the suspicion that they were being followed. It's that familiar feeling when something is nudging at you from the inside but you're not sure what it is. Things about this case were quickly becoming complicated and more muddled. Scally had the feeling that this wasn't going to be a clear-cut matter of simply helping out the Presidog. A lot more was going on in Washington D.C. and it was starting to feel increasingly like hostile territory. He noticed that Wag too was looking pensive. Yet he wasn't sure if this was because of the overall situation or whether he was nervous about meeting Tuesday again. Scally looked behind them through the taxi's rear windscreen. He was positive that a dark SUV had been following them. Then again, there were many nondescript dark SUVs around. He remembered what Thursday had said a short while before – the CIA practically runs the place. Maybe they were being trailed by the CIA. That would be normal standard practice.

A short while later, the taxi pulled up outside the *Barking Mad Diner*. Scally entered first. The diner, in typical US style with chrome fittings, had a long table-top bar with bar stools and booths by the window. It was a third-full of clients. Nothing out of the ordinary. They took a booth at the far end. Wag was looking around a little nervously. Then his dark floppy ears pricked up as soon as he saw who was approaching. His face muscles relaxed. He became the same old Wag again. Once a Wag, always a Wag, thought Scally.

"Welcome back, guys." Tuesday Adams, the waitress, was standing by their table. They both looked at her. She looked back. They knew that she knew that they now knew. It was a case of everyone knowing. This made Wag think once again of his beloved Lo-Poo. As Lo-Poo said: *If both the knower and the known knows what there is to know, then nothing needs to be said.* Wise words indeed, thought Wag. So, he said nothing.

"You don't wanna order anything – or has the cat got your tongue?" Tuesday laughed gently, then gave Wag a quick wink. "I think I know what this Wag wants. A double burger with extra chilies and topped with a huge splash of tabasco sauce. Right?"

Wag's mouth began to water. He held up his

paw. "You got me all figured out, sweetie."

"And how about I grill some extra zucchini for you to put on top of the burger?"

Wag looked Tuesday in the eyes. "I'm not a zucchini type of dude – I'm the courgette type," replied Wag with a smile.

Scally coughed into his paw. "Erm, I'll just have a chickpea burger topped with roasted sesame seeds."

"Mmm…I'll see what we can do. It's not as if we run the place," Tuesday replied with a knowing smile.

After Tuesday had left, Wag stopped smiling. "Why don't you take a trip to the loo, Scally."

"What, you need some extra relish space now?"

"No. Two dudes just walked in and sat in a booth at the back. I got a bad smell instinct about them. They're trying too hard to look and act normal. This is Washington D.C. Everyone's got an agenda in this town. You can't be normal."

"I'll check them out." Scally got up and walked the length of the diner to get to the restroom. As he passed the final booth, he gave the occupants a quick glance over. They caught his look but glanced away. They were two regular looking black Labrador Retrievers. Yet Scally had caught something about their eyes. Black. Too black. Almost as if no one was home. Scally came out of the restroom and instead of returning to the booth he took a seat at the bar. Wag knew immediately something was wrong when Scally asked Tuesday for a coffee.

"How'd you like that? I know you guys like everything with milk."

"Black. Just black. And two of them. And I don't drink coffee."

Tuesday looked up. She very slightly bent her head around where Scally was sitting. She noticed the black retrievers. "Black it is. It's a different flavor. We've not had this make of coffee here before. It's certainly not a local brew."

"I think we'll take our order to go. Can we pick it up round back?"

"Sure, no problem. I'll get it ready for you. Be careful, the coffee might burn you."

Scally nodded and returned to the booth. Wag had been on the nose. Something about them just didn't smell right. "We're taking our order to go. We're picking it up round back. We may need to make some distraction."

Wag's ears waggled. "You want a scene?" He nodded over Scally's shoulder. "There's a fire extinguisher in that glass case. I'll go make the distraction while you smash the glass, get the extinguisher, and slide it over to me. Okay?"

Wag got up and slowly strutted over to the other side of the diner. He stopped when he got to the booth

where the two black Labrador retrievers were seated.
Wag shivered then ran his paws down his own black
fur.

"Oooh, excuse me gentlemen, but I feel a little
chilly-willy-nilly. I sense a fire coming on. Ooh baby,
ooh, you got me all burning up." Wag did his waggle
dance and moved his behind with a little wag of his
tail. Then he started to sing…

Nikola Tesla, Doris Day, chemtrails, Johnnie Ray
Pearl Harbor, Hugo Chavez, Kim Jong-un, Kung Fu,
Joe McCarthy, Charlie Manson, Golden Girls,
Simpsons too,
Kazakhstan, Crimea, Ukraine, diarrhea.

Rockefellers, Goodfellas, Ninja Turtles, Rothchild,
Hong Kong, H-bomb, Pop Tarts, Robert Wagner,
Heart to Heart,
Mariah Carey, Backstreet Boys, Destiny's Child, NSYNC.

NBC, ABC, CBS, CIA,
Edward Snowden, Wikileaks, Dallas Cowboys, NSA
Whistleblowers, vaccines, world baseball, forest fires,
Postal votes, hearing aids, election fraud, no bond buyers.

You started this fire, and kept it burning, burning,
You kept igniting it with fossil fuels and cheap perfumes,
You started this fire, and kept it burning, burning…

Scally could take no more. He smashed the glass case and slid the fire extinguisher over the floor to where Wag was strutting his stuff.

Wag grabbed the extinguisher. "And now I'm putting out the fire!" he screamed as he pulled the pin and squeezed as the foam spurted out over the two Labrador retrievers. Scally jumped behind the counter and grabbed a five-liter container of cold cooking oil and threw it over the flummoxed retrievers already struggling with the onslaught of the foam attack.

Wag and Scally dashed outside amid the confusion and round to the back of the diner to where Tuesday was waiting in a blue Mustang car with the engine running. They jumped inside and sped off.

"Thank dog it's Tuesday and not another day of the week," said Wag panting and sweating. It had been quite a performance.

"Actually, it's Thursday," replied Tuesday.

"My new favorite day of the week," said Scally, grinning. "Oy, did you have to make such a song and dance about it back there, Wag?"

Wag slumped back in the seat. "I drank the cool aid, dude. The whole freaking bottle of it. Hey, Tuesday, great car you got here."

"Thanks. It's a Mustang – a 65 Shelby."

"Nice...Mustang Sally."

"No, it's a Mustang Tuesday. But no time for chitchat, we're not out of the doghouse yet. Those guys are coming up behind and I guess they're not after an encore."

"Oh, shagbasket, we've got a pair of enraged anti-foam activists on our tail. Can we shake them?" asked Wag.

"Doing my best. Time to put paw to the pedal to the metal." Tuesday swerved the car into the right turn only lane then jumped a red light to speed straight ahead. A device on top of the dashboard began to bleep and flash red.

"What does that mean?" asked Scally, leaning forward.

"It means that they're trying to jam the electrics of this car. They're aiming an electromagnetic jammer at us."

"Will it work?"

"Luckily not. This car is from 1965. No modern electrics. That's why I drive it. But…"

"But what?" asked Scally, not totally sure he wanted to hear the answer.

"They can still ram us off the road."

"Floor it then!" Scally looked behind at the dark-windowed SUV that was catching up on them. Generally speaking, Scally had a cool temperament, somewhere between concrete and hardwood tiling. It was a feature of his that he preferred it when others couldn't tell what he was thinking. After all, thinking was always a giveaway. Scally had trained himself to hide his thoughts. And Wag had soon come to learn that you just don't ask Scally what he's thinking. Scally was the last person you should ask – 'what's the plan, Stan?' So, on this occasion, Wag looked over at Scally; and Scally looked back at Wag in his customary cool fashion. And neither of them said anything. But that didn't really help matters either. Why – did you expect it would?

"If we don't outrun them in twenty doggone seconds, then we ditch the car," said Scally suddenly.

"What!?" screamed back Tuesday.

"Never get yourself boxed in. I like this car, but I'm getting the box feeling creeping up on me."

Wag started counting silently in his head. Sixteen doggone seconds remaining. He knew he'd have to be the one to tell Tuesday that time was up. Scally was right. The SUV had drawn up parallel to them and looked like it was going to try ramming them anytime soon.

"Park it behind that taxi, there," said Wag, pointing to a parked taxicab a little further up. "Do it, Tuesday – trust in Dogspeare."

"Forget Dogspeare – I trust in you," replied Tuesday as she pulled the car to a screeching halt as the SUV went racing past them, braking far too late. The three of them jumped out of the Mustang and followed Scally as he led them through the doors of a small, run-down looking movie theater. They rushed past the bored-looking clerk behind the ticket counter.

"We're season ticket holders," shouted back Wag, feeling a little bad at skimping on the payment. Then again, they were in a mad rush. Wag noticed too that on the poster board was advertised the present matinee. It was a re-showing of a classic 80s Australian film called *Dogs in Space*. That's typical, thought Wag. One of my favorite films that I haven't seen in years, and I happen to be running away from a couple of spaced-out dudes. They ran through a dark auditorium where three customers were sat watching the film. At the back, near the screen, was the door marked EXIT in a very low-lit neon green. The whole movie theater looked like it had seen better days. Wag tried to catch at least a quick glance of the film as they ran past, through the door, down a dimly lit staircase and out into a side alley.

"Ah, this place looks familiar," said Scally.

Tuesday looked at him. "You know this area?"

"No. I was just trying to sound positive." Wag smiled to himself. He knew it was Scally's tone of positive sarcasm. Not always easy to pick up.

"We're actually in China-Cat Town. It's full of Asian food restaurants. One of the best places to eat." Now that Tuesday had mentioned it, Scally was very fond of a decent miso soup. Wag was at that moment thinking of a double hamburger with extra chilies. But it wasn't an eating moment.

Although Wag had thought, just for a split second, whether they may have time to get a take-out. Then he abruptly changed his mind, knowing how revolutions are best fought on half-empty stomachs.

They ran down the alley and joined onto a larger street. The smell of food was lingering in the air. They dashed past what looked like a noodle street-seller and through a group of fashion cats who were, it seemed, discussing their latest trendy attire.

"Best to get off the main street," shouted Scally. The last thing he wanted was for them to get entangled with a bunch of feisty cats with their claws out whilst the SUV was still prowling around on their tail. They slipped into another side alley that had a few outside signs swaying gently. A rather tatty looking one read 'Chow Mein Charley.'

Wag pointed to it – "that's where we need to be." It turned out that eating actually was the better option right now. Anyone chasing them would not likely consider that those on the run had decided to take a food stop, especially so soon after being in the diner. But then again, no one really knew how Wag and Scally operated. More to the point, everything Wag and Scally did had a bit of spontaneity about it.

They each ordered a plate of stir-fried noodles, with either meat, vegetables, or seitan. Wag had the meat dish. He looked over at Scally's seitan and grunted as he grabbed at the noodles with his chopsticks.

"Y'know," he said between chews and slurps, "this whole thing is getting weird."

"What's weird is that the three of us are here calmly eating noodles whilst there's some dubious dudes on our tail – and we need to get back so we can talk with my sister."

Scally nodded. But it wasn't clear to who, or to what, he was nodding to. "Those dubious dudes will be expecting us to be on the move."

"So, we confuse them by staying put," added Wag.

Tuesday poked at her vegetables. "Is that some English logic?"

"It's roundabout logic," replied Scally. "You just don't play their game."

"Or any game for that matter." Wag waved his chopsticks at them from across the table. "Look, this whole thing's a game. The whole system is a game. Existence is a game. Here I am eating these noodles. But are they even real? Is everything here even real?"

"We're in Chow Mein Charley's place," said Tuesday with a look of impatience.

"Exactly," replied Wag with a wag of his floppy-eared head. "This is the program. It's all part of the whole game system. Yet what's important is how we choose the play the game."

"And me – am I just a game to you?"

Wag looked directly at Tuesday. "You're my game-changer, Tuesday. I know I'm here and it's because of you. And you are here because of me. Beyond that, the game hasn't been written for us yet. But I can feel that you're my game-changer." Tuesday half-blushed and half-scowled. "And yet," continued Wag, "we have to know – I mean *really* know – that all this isn't real." He stuffed another chopstick scoop of Chow Mein noodles into his mouth. "I know it all looks and feels real, but this game we're all playing is part of a much bigger program. And the more you get to realize this, the more you see the cracks."

Scally sucked some noodles into his mouth. "Well, you're certainly cracking us all up right now. Look – we're all in stitches!" He laughed as he shook his head. In many ways, he still hadn't completely got used to Wag's metaphysical-revolutionary theories.

"Whatever the game is," continued Wag, "we need to be cleverer at playing it – or we may end up as the Chow Mein."

Tuesday was impressed at Wag and Scally's deft handling of the chopsticks. But she was happy she'd chosen the fork.

Thursday was already at the house when they arrived. She had been there for some time, apparently, and getting nervous about the others. Especially about her sister. She had brought with her a pen-drive and had it plugged into her sister's laptop.

"About time! Where have you been, Tuesday?"

"At Chow Mein Charley with the boys," she replied, indicating the presence of Wag and Scally behind her.

"Any trouble?" Thursday looked concerned.

"Oh, the usual big trouble in little China. We got followed but we lost them."

"I hope so. I don't like the way things are going. It's getting hotter."

Wag wiped the sweat from his forehead. "It *is* hot in here now that you mention it. Got a beer?" Thursday frowned. Then she scowled when she saw her sister, Tuesday, giggle like a little puppy.

"We're in a bigger heat than just central heating," barked Thursday.

"Hey, let's all cool down a little." Scally trotted over and smiled sweetly at Thursday. "The main thing is that we're all together."

"And no one's dead yet," added Wag.

"Yes, Wag is right. No one is dead yet. So, show us what you got there." Scally peered over at the laptop.

Thursday relaxed a little. She showed them all the files that were now on the laptop. "This is Above Top Secret. But we *have to* tell someone. And that someone cannot be within our own agency." Thursday looked over at Wag and Scally. "Both Tuesday and I have known for some time now that there's been some irregularities going on. And we think they're coming from the inside."

"What Thursday is saying," added Tuesday, "is that we may need more days of the week on our side."

Somewhere else in the United States of Ameridog, an American Pit Bull Terrier was snarling. She was furious. And she was pacing across the carpet of her fancy interior decorated room.

"What do you mean, you lost sight of them? You're supposed to be professionals. Only professionals work for me. I don't pay amateurs. Amateurs go to drama school and die young from overdoses. I deal with professionals…or, at least I thought I did. Well?"

The two black Labrador Retrievers didn't budge or say a word. Their black eyes stared into a non-existent space.

The American Pit Bull Terrier banged her clenched paw on the table. "Of course, I don't pay you. But I did create you to be professionals. Maybe I should send you both back to the mold." Her angry, scrunched face was eyeing the Black Labradors. They didn't flinch. "Okay, I'll give you another chance. But I want those Brit dogs off my trail and out of my way – got it?!"

Now it was the turn of the two Black Labradors to show their teeth.

"Holy crapmaster!" said Wag.

"That's a shagdog humdinger," said Scally. He looked over at Thursday who smiled back at him.

"It certainly is a shagdog humdinger," she replied, with a sparkle in her eye. "But that's our suspicions to date." Thursday had been showing Wag and Scally the files on the research scientists who worked secretly for the US Canine Intelligence Agency (CIA) as well as for the National Aeronautics and Spacedog Administration (NASA). A whole page of Nazi dog scientists was listed.

"Nazi scientists now working for the CIA and NASA – that sounds about right. But the dog-cloning business is pretty distasteful." Scally scratched his terrier cheek as he glanced at Thursday to get her reaction. She knew what Scally was thinking. As Head of Operations at the bunker underneath the Strategic Foresight Consulting building, Thursday Adams was directly responsible for what was going on. Worse still, she had known about the infiltration of Nazi scientists. After all, many of them were under her command.

"And are you sure there's a parallel cloning project going on?" asked Wag.
Both Thursday and Tuesday had confessed their suspicions. Thursday had grown suspicious when she realized one of their political clones had gone missing – just disappeared.

Wag whistled through his teeth. "Nil Jiffyson. Wow – would you believe it? One of your clones is missing, and its Nil Jiffyson!" He laughed. "And all over a domestic row with his lady?"

"We don't know this," added Tuesday. "We cannot be sure – but it's a rumor we have within the CIA."

"So, let me get this all straight." Scally thought for a moment. "The CIA's clone-double of Nil Jiffyson went missing shortly after it became public news that the real Nil Jiffyson had had an affair with his intern, Tonica Doginsky? And the rumor mill suspects that the fearsome Distillery Rodbottom killed her husband, Nil, in a domestic row at home after she learned about the affair. Then she went and had his clone stolen so she could appear in public with him and not be suspected of his murder?"

Thursday and Tuesday nodded their heads.

"And," continued Scally, "you and your sister now suspect that Rodbottom has perhaps back-engineered the cloning with her own scientists and could be starting some dubious clone project?" Again, Thursday and Tuesday nodded. "That's one hell of a suspicion."

"And one dog-gone hell of a clone plot," added Wag helpfully. But it was beginning to make a little bit of sense. Maybe the Rushindogs were not involved with the clone infiltration after all. Frumpus may have an enemy much closer to home.

It was Scally's turn to grab a cold beer. It had been a mad, mad day with the CIA so far, he thought. He turned to look at Thursday. "If all this is possible, then what else is possible?"

"Everything under the moon." Wag smiled and stretched himself out on the sofa.

"Talking of the moon, there's something else I need to show you," replied Thursday. Wag and Scally knew that sounded ominous. Hanging out with Thursday and Tuesday was certainly not going to be a free lunch, whichever day of the week.

CHAPTER SEVEN

A Visit to the Moondogs

Most mornings back home in the United Kingdog, Wag and Scally had woken up with cups of tea, buttered toast, and *Dog Morrison* blasting his 'Moondance' music through the house. This morning was different. They were given mugs of black coffee (which Scally didn't drink) and pancakes, tossed very beautifully by Tuesday. Thursday was smiling as she watched her sister expertly doghandle the kitchenware. Scally knew what she was thinking. She was thinking that she was glad she didn't get the CIA role of working in the diner to monitor the street. Then again, Thursday somehow wasn't as streetwise as her sister, despite her knowledge and her charm. No – Thursday was suited to the management position. Mainly because she didn't drive a Mustang. Tuesday was a Mustang type of golden Labrador.

And Wag liked that because revolutions and Mustangs go very well together – a bit like Marmite and buttered toast. And Wag was definitely missing his Marmite. Pancakes were okay, thought Wag – but, y'know, enough is enough!

"How's the pancakes?" asked Tuesday.

"Scrum-a-licious," replied Wag licking his lips. Tuesday knew it was a Waggish exaggeration, but she didn't care. Any dude with floppy ears and the deep, dark eyes that Wag had could scrum-a-licious her pancakes any time of the day.

"Pancakes to start the day is good for the bowels," added Scally, smiling.

"Talking of bowels," said Thursday, "I think I need to take you both further into the deep dark bowels of the CIA. There's a pestilence growing down there." Thursday was dressed and ready to go. She was not a morning pancake person. Scally left his coffee on the table and leapt off his stool. He was not a morning coffee person. Or any time of the day, for that matter.

"Okay. Take us into your deep, dark bowels," said Scally, without the least hint of irony. Wag was now doubting whether he was suitably prepared for the deep bowel occasion.

There was hesitancy with Tuesday. She kept repeatedly looking over at her sister, as if trying to catch her eye to get an acknowledgement. Scally had spotted it the evening before but had put it down to nervousness.

"Look, if there's something you need to tell us?" asked Scally in a gentle, reassuring voice.

Tuesday again seemed nervous. "We're not sure. About everything the CIA is doing, I mean. We also have, erhh, well…it sounds strange, but we sometimes have lapses in our memory…"

"What my sister is trying to say," interrupted Thursday, "is that you can't trust the CIA. Even when they're supposed to be on your side. They play everyone against each other. So, trust no one from now on. Is that understood?"

"Sure." Scally nodded in agreement. It sounded reasonable enough. Wag scratched his underbelly and sniffed his paw but didn't say a word.

They pulled up outside a building in Thursday's Oldsmobile Bravada SUV. Tuesday was wishing she could pick up her Mustang from where she had dropped it off the day before, yet for now it was still too much of a risk. Scally looked up at the sign on top of the building. It read – "Radio Liberty."

Wag spotted it too. "I don't do interviews," he said with a wave of his paw. "I find that the press always misquotes me."

"Life isn't always about *you*," muttered Tuesday as the four of them climbed out of the SUV. As they did so, a passer-by gave the SUV a quick glance and then made an evil look. Tuesday shook her head. "Bloody Joe Normies," she said. "The only opinion people have these days is what the media gives to them. This country's getting like the walking dead." Wag was triply impressed as he tried to clean the pancake stain on his jacket. Scally, as normal, was impeccably attired in his smart crimson waistcoat. He looked up again at the sign. Radio Liberty, he thought. If it has got something to do with promoting liberty, then it's probably another false front for the CIA to peddle its propaganda. He wasn't far wrong. But neither was he fully right. As in all things in the United States of Ameridog, there was no clear left or right distinction – there was only those that knew and those that didn't know. Neither Wag nor Scally had any idea what was in store for them. It was going to be almost impossible for them to even keep their paws on the ground.

Thursday took them into the building and, passing the first reception, took them through to some rooms at the back where heavily armed guards scanned and gave them security passes. Wag was upset that he had to hand over his tazer. Scally had already guessed they were going to enter some deep black operation that the CIA was running, perhaps similar to their cloning one. It was obvious that Thursday and Tuesday both had authoritative jurisdiction here also.

"The Strategic Foresight Consulting is our other base of operations," said Thursday as they took a top-level security lift to the lower floors. "And Radio Liberty is our other base. They both work together. I'm the Head at Strategic Foresight. Here, I'm kinda like the Deputy." Thursday looked over at her sister and made a grimace. "But here is where I suspect things are getting blacker. When we leave the elevator, just follow me but say nothing."
The doors eventually slid open and the four of them exited into yet another dimly lit underground corridor. The walls were made of exposed rock and there was an 'echo chamber' type of feel. Wag and Scally appeared casual and relaxed as they walked alongside Thursday and Tuesday, yet they could feel a dense, subdued energy around them. It seemed like the kind of place where people didn't speak unless they had very good reason to. As if some secrets are best left unspoken.

Wag could feel the heavy energy in the pit of his stomach. Usually, he reserved that space for the final digestion of the last portions of food. But now, it was filled with the empty sounds of a hollow gong.

"The empty sounds of a hollow gong," whispered Wag to himself.

"What?" Scally turned to give his friend a quick glance.

"Oh nothing. I just thought I heard a voice saying that my stomach is filled with the empty sounds of a hollow gong."

Scally shook his head. "I think maybe you ate a pancake too much."

Thursday turned to give them both a strong look which basically meant they should leave the gong-pancake conversation for another time. They passed several more heavily armed guards who all checked their passes and, after a few words with Thursday, let them move on. Eventually they came to a thick-set arched metal doorway that needed both Thursday's and Tuesday's biometric scans to open it. The half-meter thick door mechanically opened, and they walked through into a small room. Once the arched doorway had closed behind them, a fuzzy light illumed the room. There was nothing in it. It was empty.

Wag nodded to Scally. "Here is where they try to do away with us. Could sure do with my tazer right now." Wag smiled at Tuesday. "Just kidding. I mean, I know your name technically signifies that you are the Norse god of war. But really, I don't hold it against you."

"Sure thing, little Wag. After all, a Tuesday by any other name is still a day of the week – right?" Tuesday smiled. A tickly shiver ran down Wag's spine. How he loved it when someone else quoted Dogspeare back at him.

It was Scally who noticed the elevator door in the far wall. "Going down some more?" He wasn't sure he liked the look on Thursday's face. Then he realized that her name signified the Norse god of thunder. Lucky me, he thought. I only have to deal with thunder.

The four of them stepped through what looked like an elevator door. Inside, it was almost the size of a small room.

"Just stand still and relax," said Thursday as she pressed some buttons on the wall. "Try and go with the flow." She looked over at Wag and Scally with a sly smile. Wag discreetly tried to rub his ass against the wall. It had been itching for several minutes. Within what had seemed like only a few seconds (hardly time for Wag to get a good scratch), the doors opened again. And yet there had been no sensation of movement. Scally was sure the elevator had not even started to move. He was expecting to see the same empty room again in front of them. But to his surprise he saw a large room busy with people. Wag too was a little disorientated. It was as if they had just stepped into the elevator long enough for the doors to close and open again.

"Did we get far?" asked Wag, suspiciously.

A uniformed soldier passed them as they stepped out of the elevator. "Welcome to Lunar Base,

Commander Adams." The soldier saluted and trotted off.

The two Britdog agents didn't say anything. That is, until they had arrived at the viewing room. Wag and Scally had always admired the rolling hills of Britdog, yet this view was literally out of this world.

"If this is what you're telling me it is, then it is indeed impressive," said Scally in a subdued tone.

Wag elbowed him in the ribs. "Come on, Scally – impressive? It's dog-gone mega-butt crazily crackpot amazing. Well, spank me backwards. We're either in the best movie studio in Dogwood or we're on the moon, dog dammit!" Wag whistled through his teeth. He never expected he would get to the moon. Least of all in an elevator that didn't move.

"Yes, we are on the moon. And we arrived through what's called a Jump Room," said Tuesday, with a sympathetic smile.
Wag knew that didn't make the slightest sense. But it didn't matter. If the CIA had managed to create some crazily quantum gateway to the moon, then they could call it whatever they wanted. He wasn't going to argue about silly names.

"It's the dark side of the moon. A covert group within the CIA has a base here that's not detected by any non-US satellites." Thursday was at the control panel adjusting the screen view.

"And at the dark side, it's permanently facing

away from the earth." Scally nodded to himself. A perfect hideaway. Then he saw what Thursday had been trying to show them. The pockmarked surface of the moon was not empty. There were figures moving around outside…without spacesuits…

Back at the White House, Frumpus was pacing around his Oval Office munching on jellybeans and sipping nervously on his diet coke. He had heard nothing for days from his United Kingdog friends and this made him worry. Vice Presidog Spencer was standing nearby not knowing what to say. His short cut hair made this ex-military Labrador look like part of the furniture.

"Move, damn you," barked Frumpus to his Vice Presidog. "Do something. Do a somersault or jump through hoops. Just don't stand there like a lampshade."

"Sir. We have to rely on our own intelligence. We need to be careful of all these overseas special relationships we have. We can't go to bed with everybody." Spencer was keeping calm despite feeling the grenades of anxiety well-up inside of him.

"I don't want to go to bed with everybody," snapped Frumpus as he put another pawful of jellybeans into his mouth. "I only want to go to bed with my darling Sueme without my ex-wife

Ayewanna knowing about it. Is that too much to ask?"

"Sir, with great respect. Your affair with Sueme has already caused a scandal. We need to focus on your popularity for the next election."

"Spencer, you may be a loyal dude, but you don't have one single paw on the pulse of this great nation. I have great popularity – every dog loves me. I'm the nation's top dog. I don't care what breed they are, I've got their back. You know what I say - *Make Ameridog Bark Again!*"

Spencer nodded but sighed quietly to himself. He'd heard nothing *but* that slogan recently. "Well, I sure hope we can bark louder than the clones," he muttered under his breath. At that moment, there was a knock at the door and a dog-in-black security agent ushered in Podenko, the Captain of US Presidog Guards.

Frumpus's poodle face lit up. "Ah, Podenko, just the dog I need to see. Give me a nod, Pod."

Podenko didn't like that expression one little bit. But he had forced himself to get used to it; at least whilst Frumpus was still the Presidog. "It seems our Britdog friends are collaborating with two of our CIA agents."

"And who are these agents of ours?"

"Tuesday and Thursday."

Frumpus paused. "Does the Canine Intelligence Agency give all its agents names of the week? They have more than seven agents, don't they? What would they call the eighth agent - January? The months would at least give them twelve names more."

Podenko paused. He was trying to process whether the Presidog of Ameridog was being ironic or not. He guessed not. "Sir, they are real names."

Frumpus pushed back his mop of frizzy hair. "Well, I'll be dog-whipped. What is post-modernism coming to these days, with such names. I tell you, Podenko, we're living in a post-truth world where lies are fatter than the barnacles of good old, honest fact!" Podenko and Spencer were both ex-military; as such, they knew when to straighten up and say nothing. Only their mouths gave a slight twitch. Frumpus continued to shake his head. "Post-truth world. I tell you, boys, it's all out of this world. Nothing left for it but to create a new Space Force to protect our post-truth world from above with weaponized satellites."

Podenko coughed. "Er, Sir, we already have a United States of Ameridog Space Force."

"We do? Well, I'll be double dog-whipped."

"Dogs in space without spacesuits? Now that's impressive," said Wag.

"It's also slightly disturbing," added Scally. The view they were watching was no ordinary scene.

There were figures walking around what looked to be some form of base or camp. There were several dome structures, and the figures were involved in activities across an open stretch of the moon's surface. They were wearing heavy boots, presumably to keep them weighted under some form of gravity. And they were wearing a style of protective clothing, but it was not a spacesuit – no helmet, no oxygen tank. The scene reminded Wag of a football field. There was a center patch of area that was surrounded by tall masts; some of them looked like communication towers. Others were like stadium lights. There was a hive of activity taking place both outside as well as inside the so-called Lunar Base.

Thursday had to go off to engage, as she said, in some Commander duties. Meanwhile, Tuesday was taking care of Wag and Scally. She made it clear to them – actually, very clear – that they had to stick closely with her. Any persons without Top Level clearance found wandering the base could be exterminated on sight. Wag was somewhat ruffled at the news. He fancied a good sniff around the place. Maybe even a quick pee or two in some of the least suspected places. But he got the message – this place was *certainly* not his territory. Scally gave his buddy a warning glance. He knew that the revolutionary itch was rising in his friend. Yet this was not the time for playing the Game without either knowing the new game-rules, or without having a spacesuit. Tuesday took them from the viewing platform and into a secured communications room. At least there was a pot of coffee available. Space coffee, reasoned Wag, disappointed. Scally was in a pensive mood. He was thinking about the Jump Room technology. How long had the US been using this technology? And were they the only ones with it – did the United Kingdog have a Jump Room? Certainly, *W*, Head of Dog Intelligence, had never mentioned it. The US has the high ground, he thought. They've got the highest military position. This makes Hamburger Hill look like a pimple on a buffalo's bottom. Scally knew that Thursday was taking great risk in showing them this US Lunar Base. She had craftily used their working for Presidog Frumpus as a White House protection cover for showing them this. This meant that Thursday, and also Tuesday, were deeply concerned with happenings within their own ranks. They were so concerned that they had to turn to outsiders just to share it. Didn't they trust their own people? Scally could see that Tuesday was looking concerned, despite her Golden Labrador coolness.

"What do you think, Wag?" asked Scally quietly.

Wag sniffed. "I think this space coffee tastes like strangled cat urine."

"I mean, seriously."

"Seriously, it does. But yeah, there's a whole load of mule mischief going on here that some dudes don't want the world to know about. And if those 'some dudes' find out that now we know, we could end up on their blacklist."

"So, why are the girls showing us all this?"

"They obviously want Frumpus to know about it – from us. We're the outside direct line – get it?"

Scally nodded. He got it all right. For now, because of their clone investigation, they had a private line to the Presidog's ears. Suddenly, Thursday entered and waved for them all to follow her. They exited the room, passed through a corridor, and took several flights of steps downwards. They could see that the artificial air was being maintained by a regular series of overhead air filtering valves and tubes. The atmosphere felt chilly and dry, as if being in a sealed container. They were now obviously under the surface of the moon. The steps finished at what appeared to be a train platform. Yet they could see neither train nor rails. They walked along the platform until they came to a stationary cylindrical container. Thursday pushed an exterior button and the side opened. Inside there were two seats.

"Wag and Tuesday, both of you get into this one. Scally and I will follow on."

"And I'm climbing into...what, exactly?" asked Wag in a less than enthusiastic tone.

"A vacuum pod. It's how we move around under the surface. I don't have time to explain. Jump in. It's completely safe," said Thursday slightly irritated.

Sure, thought Wag. Any pod under the surface of the moon would be safe. Why wouldn't it be? And if you screamed out here, would anyone hear you?

Wag didn't have much time for thinking more about the screaming, as the pod he was strapped into was hurtling – or rather, screaming – along its destined route through smoothly cut bore holes within the moon's interior. And before any of them could get their minds back together they had already arrived at the place they were supposed to arrive at. Fast, super-fast, thought Scally. Phheww-flipping-Swayze-Dirty-Dog-Dancing fast, thought Wag. Both were impressed and slightly dizzy. They followed Tuesday and Thursday down an extended corridor and into a large rock-cut interior chamber. Inside the large chamber were several moon buggy vehicles. Thursday showed them to where the moon suits were available.

"Suit-up," she said. "We're going for a ride."

Never mind viewing the moon from afar - should dogs ever travel across the surface of the dark side of the moon? This was Scally's thinking as the moon buggy bounced over potholes and sped across a plateau. Wag was loving it. He was on the freaking moon's surface. But then he realized he wouldn't be able to take a pee, and his enthusiasm dipped slightly. Yet the sight and the whole atmosphere was both surreal and awesome. It was like being on a Stanley Dogbrick movie set. The silence was eerie and although they were moving at speed, the surroundings hardly seemed to change, as if they were moving but going nowhere fast. And, more than anything, the blackness surrounded them overhead. So, this *really is* the dark side of the moon, thought Scally. It felt totally isolated. And this made him shiver. Wag was also strangely silent, as if engulfed by the enormity of the occasion.

The buggy, with Tuesday and Thursday sitting upfront, reached a high vantage point and stopped. Thursday pointed into the distance. Her lips moved within the helmet, but nothing could be heard. She clicked on her mic switch.

"We're on a private, secure channel. We have to be out here to talk securely. Everything within the Lunar Base is monitored. In fact, everything that happens between the moon and the Earth, including everything on the Earth, is monitored."

Scally nodded. He understood. The whole world, and more, was now under incredible surveillance.

"Top dog secret," added Wag. He was still

impressed with the view. Thursday pointed again, out over the ridge and into the distance. This time when they looked, they could all see it. There was another set of buildings and a matrix of what looked like tall antennas that were all connected to each other.

"Another part of your Lunar Base?" asked Scally.

Thursday shook her head. "We're not alone on the moon."

"Dog aliens?!" Wag called out with renewed enthusiasm. Then he noticed in the distance a large flag that was unflapping in the non-wind. A golden and white flag.

"No," replied Thursday. "It's the Vatican. They have a Vatican City in Rome, and another one here on the moon too." For the first time in a very long, long time, both Scally and Wag's jaws dropped simultaneously as if synchronized.

"And…all the antennas they have here?" asked Scally finally.

"They're searching for dog aliens," replied Thursday without smiling.

Thursday then turned 180 degrees and pointed in the opposite direction. There was another set of buildings with some unusual outdoor activity. This time it was Scally who first noticed the flag.

He grabbed a telescopic device from the buggy and looked more closely. His facial hairs twitched. He looked again, closely, just to be sure. Yes, he recognized its colors immediately. His chest tightened up and he felt as if his stomach had just dropped to the claws of his toe paws. This was not good.

The dark side of the moon suddenly got a lot darker. And out of that darkness came two strange moon buggies heading straight for them.

"Buckle up!" screamed Thursday through the headset microphone, which Wag thought odd since they had been buckled up the whole time. The buggy lurched forward as Thursday stepped on the throttle and swung it around. They sped off down the inclination as the two other buggies came at them fast from the direction of the Vatican compound.

"I guess they don't like us watching them," shouted Wag from the back of the buggy as it jumped around in the low gravity. Luckily, they had a head start and the downward slope in front of them.

"They don't usually send out scouts," shouted back Thursday. A light started flashing on the buggy dashboard. Tuesday pointed to it and nudged her sister. "They're trying to hail us – to communicate."

"Should we respond?" asked Tuesday. Thursday responded in her own way by swinging the buggy to the left and then making a dash over a flat stretch of the moon's surface.

"I thought the moon was neutral territory?" shouted Scally as he held on tight to the buggy's frame.

"This is no dog's land that we're in right now. Need to get back to Ameridog territory – and fast!"

Wag watched, in an odd state of detachment, as he saw the two chasing buggies try to pull up parallel to them. He looked over his shoulder and the sight made him blink, three times. The other buggies were being driven by dogs without the proper spacesuits, and no helmets!

"Yikes – moondogs!" yelped Wag. He looked again. Sure enough. And they looked to be Greater Swiss Mountain Dogs. He relayed back the information.

"They're the Vatican's Swiss Guard," replied Thursday. "But they shouldn't be coming out this far. We must have startled them."

We startled *them*? Wag was sure it was the other way around, yet he wasn't going to argue the point. He fell back into his strapped seat and looked up into the blackness. He thought that there would have been more stars. He then realized how weird it all was. Never in a million dog years did he think he would one day be strapped to the backseat of a moon buggy being chased over the surface of the moon. Never say never, he thought to himself.

"Never say...what?" asked Tuesday. It seemed Wag had been thinking aloud again. He decided to keep his thoughts as quiet as he could as their own buggy struck across the path of one of the other buggies causing it to break to a sharp halt. They swerved back on course and continued at a fast pace until they could see the lights of the Ameridog Lunar Base. The other buggy had also halted. They were now on safe territory.

Sweating like a pig in a dog's moon suit is not recommended, thought Wag to himself.

"What's that about a pig?" asked Tuesday.

Damn! Wag slapped his helmet.

Scally gave a deep sigh. "We don't have much time," he said, aloud.

CHAPTER EIGHT

Operation Staplepin

They had returned to the US Lunar Base after their outside adventure and soon the four of them were de-suited and back drinking space coffee in a closed, private lounge. Thursday was looking apprehensive. And so was her sister, Tuesday. Scally understood the situation. The more that they, Wag and Scally, knew about these projects and secret operations, the more they were at risk – all of them. Thursday had taken a great risk herself in securing top level clearance and showing them this. Both Thursday and Tuesday could get into serious trouble for becoming too involved with two Britdog agents. And Wag and Scally also knew that they could be in serious trouble back home for knowing what they now know.

"How many others back at Dog Intelligence know of this?" asked Wag. "Do you think *W* knows?

And Queenie?"

Scally shook his head. "If Queenie knows, then I'm a shortbread biscuit. I doubt it. I'm not even sure if *W* knows about the secret base they have here on the moon. I think this goes even higher than Dog Intelligence."

Wag whistled through his teeth. "Oh, bonedigger! Then we're standing deep in turd. No one else can know that we know there is a secret Britdog base on the moon."

Scally looked over at Wag with a pale face. "I don't think we're dealing with a Britdog base."

Wag tilted his head. "I thought you said the flag was the colors of St. George, the white with a red cross?"

"Yeah," replied Scally, biting his lip. "But I also saw an upturned sword in the top left corner. That's the City of London flag. And it's a corporation. This is a private enterprise outside the jurisdiction of the United Kingdog."
Tuesday and Thursday looked at one another. The Vatican City on the dark side of the moon. Now they realized that it was not United Kingdog as they had been led to believe but the City of London with a lunar base also.

Scally turned to Thursday. "And Commander Adams, where do your orders originate from?"

"Washington, District of Columdog."
Scally was beginning to see a pattern now.

Wag smacked his lips together. "Damn, this space coffee sure does taste like a strangled cat's urine."

"You've already said that!" called over Tuesday from the chair opposite.

"If I repeat myself, it's because something is true. I only tell lies once."

Scally was strutting around the room. He seemed to be unusually nervous. "First things first – we need to get out of here. Being deep into space territory is dangerous. If anything should happen to us here, no one would ever know. We need to get back into close quarters. And that also means making contact with Frumpus, asap." Thursday and Tuesday both agreed.

Wag nodded his head solemnly. "No one hears you scream in space. I've heard that said in the movies so many times it's become a modern truth."

"No one's going to scream – come on!" said Scally, looking over at Thursday to take the lead.

They were halfway down the corridor when they were stopped by two heavily armed security guards.

"Commander Adams, you have to come with us. We need all senior ranking officers in the control room right away. We have a situation. There are some issues with Pope-1 Lunar Base."

Thursday knew she didn't have a choice. She nodded to her sister. "Take them to the Jump

Room. I'll meet you back on terra firma. I'll need *time* to look into this situation." She then went off with the security guards. Tuesday led the way to the Jump Room and breathed a sigh of relief once the large doors were closed. She pressed one of the large buttons.

"Terra firma?" asked Wag.

"It's Latin for solid earth," said Tuesday.

"Why didn't she say so?" Wag shrugged.

"She was giving me a code. She was saying there is firm terror on the way, and that she would buy us time to get out of here and get safe."

"Then let's do it," added Scally, looking concerned. He didn't like the idea of leaving Thursday behind.

The large doors opened. And yet it felt like they had never moved. It has to be the best elevator in the world, thought Wag. This time no one else heard him. They exited the Radio Liberty building and into bright sunlight. The sun stunned their eyes as if it were a laser hitting them rather than shimmering rays. For a while, the three of them sat on a low wall by the sidewalk as they gathered their senses. Shortly, Scally took the courage to look up into the clear blue sky. He found what he was looking for. Over to the West was the white silhouette of the moon, hovering high in the sky like an observing eye. Scally felt sad, knowing how Thursday was still up there, on the other side of the moon. The dark side of the moon. He really wanted to be with her. He dropped his head in his hands and breathed deeply. He knew Thursday was strong and competent. She was Commander Adams, after all. But still…

Scally looked up to see Wag standing several meters away besides a fast-food stand. Wag turned and came back with three hotdogs in his hands, offering them to Scally and Tuesday.

"I put extra mustard on them to give us the kick we need. And plenty of fried onions too. No point in feeling low when there's a hot dog to be had." Wag stuffed the hot dog into his mouth, wiping away the mustard dripping onto his chin. "I just don't get it, why do they call pavements here sidewalks?" he said, turning to Tuesday. "I mean, no one walks sideways, do they?"

Tuesday blinked and looked over at Scally.

Scally smiled back. "It's his distraction technique. He does it to get my mind off something. He's a top-dog psychologist really – you just wouldn't know it."

Tuesday felt a warm shiver ripple over her back fur. Then she felt a second shiver in her backbone. "Come on, we need to go. I've got a spare set of keys for Thursday's car. Follow me."

The Oldsmobile Bravada SUV moved through the traffic with haste. They were heading to the White House and for a meeting with Presidog Frumpus. No more time to waste. Tuesday turned on the radio to give them some music to calm their minds. An eerie, hypnotic tune began playing. Wag's ears picked up.

"Ah, I love this song. Turn it up. It's Dog Floyd – the song *Us and Them* from their album 'Dark Side of the Moon.'" Too late. Wag's words had left his mouth before his mind could consider them.

Frumpus was pacing around the oval office. Vice Presidog Spencer was eyeing him nervously.

"It's us and them, Spencer. It's us and them… or, them and us. But it's not us both together." Frumpus was frustrated, scratching his white mop of hair. "What if I wake up one morning, look at my gorgeous self in the mirror, and find that I'm a clone – can you imagine that? What would I do then, as a clone of myself? Dog dammit, this goes far beyond the dog biscuit. This is war, Spencer."

"Yes, Sir. We're at war with an invisible enemy."

"They're not invisible, you idiot! We know what they look like. They look exactly like us – they're our clones! Look, I don't want to wake up one morning and find that I've changed into my own enemy. I don't want to be my own worst enemy."

Spencer nodded dutifully. "Certainly not, Sir. You certainly do not want to be your own worst enemy."

"I'm feeling frazzled, Spencer, I tell you. I'm fracked and frazzled, and this isn't good for my complexion. I need a diet cola." Frumpus pressed a button on his desk and shortly one of his aides arrived with a bottle of diet cola on a tray.

"Presidog, Sir. What about those intelligence agents from our ally United Kingdog – have they unearthed any bones in this mystery?"

Frumpus pouted and rubbed his behind on the arm of the sofa. "Nothing from those guys. What are they doing, moon gazing? We need to get all our paws onto this one. I'm running this Cabinet on a skeleton staff. I can't trust half the guys and gals working here."

An aide entered the Oval Office with news that Britdog agents Wag and Scally were at the gates of the White House, asking to see the Presidog.

"About time! Well, let them in. Don't just stand there on four legs."

"Presidog, Sir," said the aide, "they also have one of our CIA agents with them. A certain Tuesday Adams."

"I don't care what day of the week she is – let her in too. This is our moment of reckoning."

Frumpus slapped his paws together then reached for his jar of colored jellybeans.

Not a long time later, in the War Room bunker...

The atmosphere was tense. The large, solidly constructed bunker room, with its reinforced concrete nuclear-proof walls, was almost silent. Almost. Frumpus was tapping his paws on the large conference table trying not to look, or sound, nervous. Podenko, the Captain of US Presidog Guards, was standing by his side. As a German Shephard hunting dog, he was used to tense situations. And he always knew that this moment would come. He had just hoped it would always be later rather than now.

"That's correct, Sir. We do have a secret Lunar base on the dark side of the moon." Podenko kept a rigid look.

Frumpus ruffled his paws through his mop of hair. "And why wasn't I told about this, Pod?"

Podenko didn't like being called Pod. But there was little he could do. He hid his irritation calmly. "It was secret, Sir."

"And don't I get to know secrets too? I'm the Presidog of this great United States of Ameridog. I'm going to make this great country of ours bark again."

Podenko had heard this refrain countless times. It had long ceased being even remotely amusing – or inspiring. "Well, to be honest, Sir, the Lunar Base is top, top secret. And you only have top secret clearance. We didn't know you wanted top, top-secret clearance when you asked for top secret clearance."

Frumpus cleared his throat. "I didn't know there was a top, top-secret clearance. I thought that top secret was the top. How was I to know?"

Podenko made a gesture of a slight shrug. "And how were we, the military, to know that you wanted top, top-secret clearance?"

"Well – I do now!"

"I will confer with the top military chiefs and get back to you, Sir." Podenko marched out of the war room.

Scally was impressed at the non-transparency of the political hierarchy. He had always thought that politicians were ludicrously inept. Now, seeing that they had many degrees of compartmentalization and 'need-to-know' secret categories, his estimation had moderately increased. Wag was neither impressed nor interested. His estimation of politicians had always been lower than that of plumbers. After all, people need plumbers in their lives much more than they need politicians. That was just a basic and irrefutable fact.

"Mr Presidog, Sir," said Tuesday. "We have reason to believe that my sister, Commander

Thursday Adams, is in danger on the Lunar Base."

Frumpus frowned. "But isn't she one of ours? I mean, you're both working for the Canine Intelligence Agency, our very own CIA, right?"

"That's the thing, Sir. There are factions within factions."

"You mean, like in mathematics? Mathematics was never my strong point. Neither was geography, or French. But I did great in the cookery classes."

Tuesday paused. Scally came over and whispered in her ear.

"Oh, no Sir, not fractions – I'm talking about *factions!*"

Frumpus held up his paws. "Tomato, tomartoe; potato, potarto – what's the difference? Why are we trifling over letters here? This is serious stuff, Thursday."

"It's Tuesday, Sir," said Tuesday, biting her lip.

"Really, I thought today was Friday?"

"My name, Sir. My name is Tuesday, not Thursday. Anyway, I'm talking about factions." She stopped herself. "Erm, I mean, different groups. There are baddy groups within the goody groups."

Frumpus almost jumped out of his seat. "Spank my badger! Are you ser-*i-ous*? We got baddies in the CIA too? And clones? We got clones?"

Tuesday sighed. "Probably, Sir."

"Oh, infectious bat dung! It's worse than I

thought. That means we may have to get sniffing the behinds of everyone in the CIA. Where's my Vicy, Spenser, when you need him?"

Tuesday backed away, as diplomatically as she could. Then, from a safe distance, she attempted to tell Frumpus about Operation Stablepin. As Frumpus listened, he was aghast.

"Those sniveling, butt-creeps," he said when Tuesday had finally finished telling what she knew.

By the time Podenko had returned, Frumpus's whitish poodle face had turned red with anger – or embarrassment – or a mixture of the two.

"Podenko!" yelled Frumpus, "am I top, top secret or not? If not, you're fired!"

"Yes, Sir. The top military chiefs have agreed to give you top, top secret clearance."

"Great," replied Frumpus, now somewhat a bit more relaxed. "Who are these top military chiefs anyway?"

"Err, sorry Sir, I cannot tell you that."

"Why not?" demanded Frumpus.

"You'll need top, top, top-secret clearance for that."

Frumpus sighed. "You guys will be my demise. Anyway, we got other more important matters to deal with. What's with this Operation Staplepin?" Podenko breathed deeply as he looked over at Tuesday and the others.

"He had to know," said Tuesday. She was right. Frumpus had to know, sooner or later. In fact, it should have been sooner. Podenko sat down and pulled out his electronic cigar.

"Sorry, no vaping here. Or anywhere in the White House."

Podenko grimaced, put his e-cigar away and popped a chewing gum in his mouth. "After the second big war," he said, obviously choosing his words carefully for Frumpus to understand, "we took the technology from the defeated Deutschdogs. Operation Staplepin was an operation to bring over to Ameridog the top German Shepard dog scientists and to place them into our institutions. Basically, these Deutschdog scientists helped to develop our own rocket ships, weaponry, missile technology. Even NASA has been run by one of these German Shepard dog scientists."

Frumpus's jaw dropped. "And...and...our Ameridog Space Force?"

"Yup," replied Podenko with a nod. "We wouldn't have a US Space Force without Deutschdog technology. And many of these scientists are on our secret Lunar Base right now."

"And what are these traitors doing?"

"Sir – they are not traitors. We brought them over to work for us. We gave them Ameridog citizenship. They're loyal to us now. And they're developing Moondogs."

"Moondogs?" Frumpus's face was a blank.

"Sir. These are genetically modified dog soldiers as part of an experiment to create bodies that can withstand the space environment without the need for the usual spacesuits. Neither do they need to breath oxygen. They can survive in space without the normal protection."

"You mean, we're talking about more clones here?" said Frumpus, scratching his chin.

"Yes, Sir. Basically. They are cloned dog super-soldiers."

"And why? So they can walk on the moon saving oxygen?"

"With respect, Sir. This is a top, top-secret experiment aimed at preserving the future of the United States of Ameridog."

"And how is that, Pod?"

Podenko coughed into his paw. "By allowing us to explore further into space. To secure our future, Sir."

"Far-thinking. I guess this goes much further than each Presidog and their four-year elections?" Podenko nodded.

"Are we the only ones doing this? On the moon?"
Podenko was silent.

"Speak up, Pod!" demanded Frumpus.

"Sorry, Sir. That information is above my pay grade."

"But who's paying you?"

"Tell him, Pod!" came a shout from further down the table. They all turned to look at Wag. "Oh, come on. It's painful listening to you guys talking in monosyllables. Even G.I. Joe action figures say more when you pull their strings. Pod – tell him about Vatican City and the United Kingdog having their bases on the moon too."

Frumpus groaned. Podenko looked away nervously, as if seeking for a stray fly to distract him from the situation. Wag raised his dark eyebrows to the great dog in the sky. What a palaver, he thought. Then he remembered the words of the wise Lo-Poo, his favorite philosopher. It was Lo-Poo who had said: *never create a mud bath that you are not later willing to wash in yourself.*

Tuesday stepped forward. "With respect, Sir – we need a plan."

"We do?" asked Frumpus.

"Most certainly. We need to get to the heart of the matter."

"What our illustrious colleague is saying," interrupted Scally, "is that we need to know just who exactly is behind the clones in the White House. And we might have an idea of who it could be. We suspect that the same person also has ties with the CIA and may even be conducting covert black operations within the CIA. And so, as they say, find out who's behind the clones, then you find the bones."

"What he means is," called out Wag, "find the cloner, get the boner."

"And we have a plan," added Scally.

"We do?" asked Frumpus, even more bewildered than the first time.

"We do," replied Scally.

"We do?" Tuesday looked puzzled. It was now several hours later, and they were all back at Tuesday's house. "Why didn't you tell me?"

Scally shrugged. "I hadn't thought of it until just now. I needed to get the ball rolling otherwise we would have been in that bunker until the air ran out. Besides, I needed to get inspired."

"And is that how you Britdogs get inspired – by telling lies?"

"It wasn't a lie. It was a forward-thinking proposal. I was forward proposing to the plan that I will soon have." Scally smiled and took a gulp on his bottle of beer.

Wag was in the kitchen trying to fasten his apron strings. "Hey, Tuesday, is this Michael Hasselhoff apron the only one you got?'

"It's the *Hoff*, Wag. Don't knock the *Hoff*."
Whatever you say, thought Wag. After all, he was willing to compromise a little when it came to a US hotdog like Tuesday. He really was a sucker for the golden Labradors. He got the oil all hot in the pan

and then threw in the chopped onions before adding the steaks along with a bunch of red chilies. Then he glanced over at the vegetables with a quizzical look.

Wag slammed the plates on the table. "What do you think?"

"Looks like it's up to your usual standard," agreed Scally.

"And mine, Wag? You know I'm not a steak with chili kind of gal."

Wag came back from the kitchen with another plate and placed it carefully in front of Tuesday. "Tofu and vegetables with pine nuts and coriander. All cooked in a light sesame oil."

"Darling. You're one hell of a…"

"Revolutionary. One hell of a revolutionary," interrupted Wag, finishing the sentence for her. "And I'm only soft underneath. So, you know where to tickle me." Then Wag noticed the look on Scally's face. "Oh, sorry buddy. I almost forgot about Thursday. She'll be back soon. She's a smart cookie."

"Yes," replied Scally softly as he ate his food.

Scally sipped on his beer whilst the food was digesting inside. Between thinking of Thursday and thinking of his plan, his mind was distracted. He had promised to tell Frumpus the details of the plan in the morning. He needed to sleep on it. Plans are often best thought out in sleep when the stomach is digesting the food from the night before. He picked up a fresh chili from the empty plate and absent mindedly popped it into his mouth. Okay, he thought – that certainly was not the best thing to do. Water!

Wag came dashing over with a glass of water whilst still wearing his *Hoff* apron from washing the dishes. Scally smiled to himself. Yeah, that was it. Now he had the plan. Still, I'll sleep on it, he thought.

CHAPTER NINE

Undercover at the White House

The plan had already been agreed upon and put into motion when two days later, Thursday stepped through the door. It was a very welcome surprise.

Tuesday leapt into the air and hugged her sister. Scally dashed over in a diplomatic half-jog trying to look as casual as possible. Wag watched from a distance as his old buddy also gave Thursday a welcoming hug. He didn't want to intervene and spoil the moment.

"You're back, sis!" cried Tuesday joyfully. Thursday was still a bit weak on her feet. Scally and Tuesday helped her to the sofa. Scally looked at her suspiciously.

"I'm fine," she said, brushing it off. "I'm just a bit tired, that's all."

Scally noticed a bruising on her shoulder. "Did they hurt you?"

"Me? I'm their Commander," replied Thursday, trying to sound humorous. "Well," she continued after a pause, "they injected me with a truth serum and interrogated me."

"What!?" Scally was angry. "They crossed the line. No more mister nice guys – hey, Wag?"

Wag was rubbing down his paws. "Let me taze them – all of them!"

"No, no," said Thursday waiving her paws. "It's what they regularly do. CIA agents are regularly tested with truth serums to check their loyalty. No one believes anyone in this business."

"It's true," added Tuesday with a sad look on her face. Thursday also looked concerned. Scally came over with a glass of water. Thursday drank it quickly. She then asked for something stronger. After she had drank that she turned to Scally.

"I think they may suspect something," she said, with a tone of frustration. She rubbed her shoulder where it obviously still hurt.

"They? And who are *they*?" asked Scally, still feeling angry.

"Oh, well, *they* are those who give the orders up there," she said pointing to the sky. "And I also suspect they give many of the orders down here on the ground too. We never see them – not face-to-face anyway. We only know them as '*The Council of Nine.*'

They operate secret black ops within the CIA that even most of the CIA don't know about."

"And have you ever counted them?" asked Wag. "Are you sure there's only nine of them?"

Thursday shook her head. "Like I said, we never see them. We just hear them behind the screens."

"Behind the screens?" asked Scally.

"Yes, we go into a screening room. We get our programs given to us there. But...but..." Thursday hesitated and threw a quick glance to her sister.

"But what?" Scally put his paw on her arm to encourage her.

"We've...I mean, I have been wanting to get out of this for a long time. All the programs we get given to us. It confuses me at times." She looked downcast. "I hope I haven't put any of you guys in jeopardy."

"Well, this Council of Nine *may* suspect something," said Scally, sympathetic to Thursday's situation. "But all they *can* know is that Frumpus is suspicious over the cloning. And the fact that he still thinks the Rushindogs are involved, is a good distraction. They can't know about our plan."

"What's *our* plan?" asked Thursday, looking surprised.

"Exactly. It's just been hatched." Scally gave her a cheeky wink. But he knew they needed to tread carefully from now on. He didn't like the sound of the screens and the programs that Thursday had mentioned. It sounded eerily close to a type of hypnotism.

The mansion house loomed large on the lakeside. A car was pulling up at Edgewater Ranch by Lake Eerie. The visitor had first to pass through a heavily armed security gate and drive past an array of CCTV cameras. As the visitor got out of the car, they noticed a drone buzzing nearby overhead.

The double doors opened onto a large porch with an impressive lake view. At the far end of the porch sat a squat, heavy-set American Pit Bull Terrier drinking from a glass with an umbrella.

"Distillery, we have news for you." The American Pit Bull Terrier grunted as the General came forward. 'And must you have a drone over the front door?'

"Can't be too careful – it's a dog-eat-dog world," grunted Distillery before she slurped the rest of the drink. "Okay, what ya got for me, General?"

"We've truth-interrogated one of our agents and we've learned that Frumpus knows about the clones."

Distillery growled. "That chump wouldn't know a clone from a bone. Anyway, he was bound to find out sooner or later. How much does he know, or suspect?"

"It seems, Madam," said the General respectfully, "that Frumpus believes Glutin is behind it all."

The American Pit Bull Terrier gave out a snort. "That silly turnip-head. He can hardly run a bath, never mind run a country. He doesn't play ball. This country needs us elites to run it, not grassroots popularizers. What you say, General?"

The General coughed into his paw. "Yes, Madam. We need strong leadership."

"Exactly my point – exactly." Distillery looked pleased with herself. "Make sure that Frumpus gets the message we need him to get. Tell your people to feed him more of this Rushindog business. We'll create the next Rushingate scandal for turnip-head!" Distillery broke out into muffled grunts as she spat onto the wooden porch decking.

Wag was flipping breakfast pancakes again. He was loving this. "I told you, I'm perfect for the role!" he shouted back.

Scally chuckled to himself. It was true. If anyone could go undercover as a waiter, it would be Wag. He had that non-committed, disinterested look of a waiter. Ever since teaming up with Tuesday and Thursday, all four of them had been staying together at Tuesday's place. Scally had said it was best to stick together for the co-plotting. Wag had grinned at this reasoning, as he picked the bedroom next door to Tuesday. Co-plotting, he thought, was a decent enough way to express it. And as for the rest, Tuesday could sure teach them both a thing or two about serving food and drinks, especially after all her hours working at the Barking Mad Diner. Yet it was too dangerous to take either Tuesday or Thursday along with them to the White House dinner, as they were known CIA operatives. It would be too risky. What if someone spotted them? Instead, it was planned that Tuesday and Thursday would stay out of sight and be connected to Wag and Scally through electronic surveillance. They would have eyes and ears on the ground from a distance, while the boys did the legwork – or paw work – on the ground.

It had been agreed. A grand White House dinner was arranged for the following week that Frumpus had organized, it was said, as a hasty celebration for the anniversary of the assassination of Abradog Lincoln. Frumpus announced a temporary truce in political in-fighting and for all parties and politicians to come together. He had invited past presidogs Nil Jiffyson, Geegee Bushtail, Bo-Ma, and their wives. It would be hard – or rather, politically hard – for these **VIDs** (very important dogs) to refuse such an elite invitation. As it is said in Washington D.C., you can't miss an elite gathering, even if it's your own funeral. Frumpus was sure they would all attend, even though he was not particularly looking forward to the event. He had been persuaded into it by Scally mostly. The agents from United Kingdog had assured Frumpus that they suspected someone closer to home was involved in the clone affair. Yet for now, Frumpus was told to stick vigorously to the idea that Glutin and the Rushindogs were the culprits. The more he could convince the others on this, the more space, and opportunity, it would give them. If the real culprits were convinced that Frumpus and his team were looking elsewhere, then they might be more complacent in their activities. Wag and Scally were hoping for a sign. Or a slip-up.

"Are you sure you're up for this?" Scally gave Thursday a sympathetic look. Scally was still not sure if Thursday had fully gotten over her recent ordeal. And not just that. The other evening, Wag had quietly whispered in his ear. Was Thursday completely recovered, Wag had asked? Or rather, had Thursday been compromised in some way?

"I hate to say this to you buddy," Wag had said, "but we need to be careful with *everyone* now. Remember, these dudes in Washington are the types that mess with your minds. You get me? They do psychological operations here. These are the elites of Psy-Ops." Wag had been deadly serious.

"And should I be careful with you, then?"

Scally had replied. "After all, you often act weird and brainwashed."
Wag had grinned at that comment. Scally knew his buddy well. Anything other than weird was just not the Wag he knew. And as for brainwashed – Wag had the best brain defenses in the dog-gone world.

The morning of the White House dinner engagement arrived and the four of them left Tuesday's house and headed for the White House in a discreet Duber-Dog taxi driven by a shaggy-haired English Sheepdog.

"Hey, haven't picked up many English tourists recently," said the driver as Wag and Scally climbed into the taxi with Tuesday and Thursday.

"How did you know we were Britdogs?" asked Scally.

"Easy. You guys opened the door for the girls and then stroked down your ears before entering. That's an English thing. Love you guys!"
Scally made a mental note of it. Don't stroke down the ears.

"Why are you here then and not back in Britdog?" asked Wag.

"Ah, I'm wanted for tax-paw evasion. Those damn taxes will be the death of us. I'm not sure what's worse over there, the tax-paws or the Britdog Broadcasting Corporation!" The shaggy-haired driver gave out a deep, throaty laugh.

The Duber-Dog taxi drove up the street leading to the White House, now named as *Dog Lives Matter Plaza*, and finally dropped the four tourists off at Lincoln Memorial. It was the arranged pick-up place for their rendezvous. And, thought Scally, an appropriate place given it was the anniversary of the assassination of Abradog Lincoln. At the appointed time, a large black SUV with blackened windows pulled up across from the memorial. Thursday looked nervously at her sister.

"Don't worry," reassured Scally. "These are the dogs-in-black that work for Frumpus. They're our escort to get through the back door of the White House."

Once inside, Wag and Scally were taken into the catering rooms to get dressed up and to mingle with the staff. They were introduced as two new replacements for Jiffy and Juanko that could not turn up. "What's up with Jiffy and Juanko?" asked the catering manager. Wag pulled one of his 'smashed and sloshed faces' that the manager understood immediately. No more needed to be said – or not said. The manager got them suited up and sent off to the kitchens. On their way, Wag and Scally made a detour into a side room where two of Frumpus's security agents got them wired up. They had stealth microphones tucked under their jackets that could pick up the tiniest of whispers. Then they both were given special issue glasses that had cameras installed with heat sensor capability. Now Tuesday and Thursday both had eyes and ears on the ground through Wag and Scally.

The CIA agents were secretly installed in an upper room just above the main dining area. They were seated in front of screens that relayed the vision from the surveillance glasses worn by Wag and Scally. Frumpus popped into the room suddenly with a broad smile.

"Hello, ladies," he said in an annoyingly pompous tone.

"We're CIA agents, not ladies," replied Tuesday.

"And you should be getting ready to greet your guests, Mister Presidog," added Thursday. "Oh, and play it cool, Sir. We need authenticity."

Frumpus combed back his droopy mop of poodle hair with his paw. "Authenticity is my name. And coolness is my game." He turned around and trotted out.

"Are we doomed?" Tuesday looked at her sister.

"Nah. He's actually an okay guy. He just plays himself too much."

The White House was becoming lively. Large luxury cars had been pulling up one after the other. A long line of VIDS – Very Important Dogs – were streaming into the lavish reception area. Glasses were filled and voices rose amid the clinking and pouring of drinks. Wag was loving his role as a waiter. Technically, he was a catering service provider, but that didn't stop him from just being a regular waiter to a host of pretentious stuck-up dogs. Wag served the drinks and smiled, his large black floppy ears waggling as he did so. He was hoping to fool them by playing the fool, to lull them into a false sense of security. It was a basic spy 101 type of behavior. He'd learned it well as a young pup by watching Detective Colomdog movie repeats on daytime TV.

Scally, meanwhile, was attempting to be more backroom type of sleuth. He had taken to directing the other waiters so he could move from front of house serving to back of house organizing. He wanted to check out the whole operation. Thursday was continually within his ear, speaking closely to him. He liked that. If he admitted it, it made his Yorkshire Terrier fur vibrate a little. He wouldn't tell her that though.

Wag was grooving and smooching through the crowd, offering glasses of champagne, wine, lemonade, and iced tea.

"Iced tea is for pajama-wearing bedwetters,"

whispered Wag quietly. He heard Tuesday giggle through the microphone in his ear. He liked that. They were on the same page. And it had a lot of cool writing on that page – Wag was sure of it.

There was a sudden hush in the room as everyone turned toward the main entrance. And in strolled Geegee Bushtail, the 43rd Presidog of Ameridog, a tricolored Beagle, with a silly grin on his face. His wife, on the other hand, was looking much more sophisticated. But Geegee Bushtail just kept on grinning to everyone who came up to them as fawning well-wishers.

"The main players are arriving," whispered Thursday. Scally took a drinks tray and made his way from the kitchens to the Reception Hall. He was just in time to see Bo-Ma, the 44th Presidog, entering the hall with his wife. Scally looked him over from a distance. He recognized his breed. Hard to pin down at first, as some of these breeds have dubious birth origins. Yeah, Scally recognized Bo-Ma as a Portuguese Water Dog. It was the type of breed that looks cute and harmless, yet they hide a sneaky agenda. They are loyal to their masters, however. He then noticed that Wag was wandering over to offer Bo-Ma and his wife a drink. Take it easy, Scally whispered under his breath. Don't blow this game.

"Don't blow the game," whispered Tuesday into Wag's ear. "Be a cool Wag for me, will ya?"

Wag felt tickled. He approached Bo-Ma as

formal as he could, given his natural, in-built slouch. "A drinky for you, Sire"?

Bo-Ma looked at Wag the waiter, and then smiled. "That's an interesting twang you have there. You're not from around these parts, are you?"

Wag held his breath and counted to three, so as to accomplish his professional pregnant pause. "No, Sire, I be not from around these parts. May your good self be entertained with a drink?"

Bo-Ma took two drinks from the tray and smiled back, obviously trying to place the accent of the waiter. He seemed slightly amused and bemused at the same time.

"Here's looking at you, kid," Wag replied as he bowed and turned away.

Wag and Scally heard in their ears the deep sighs of Tuesday and Thursday.

"Here's looking at you, kid. What are you trying to do – be Bogart to Bo-Ma's Bergman? Ahhh…."

"Stay cool. Wag is on the ball," whispered Wag to his listeners. "Wag is a prowling. He's on the beat. He's hit the floor." Wag didn't have chance to say another word as everyone turned and a muffled shuffling of paws could be heard. The sound of expectation. Or of hesitancy?

The whole reception area fell into a hush as she walked through the door. The American Pit Bull

Terrier strolled into the room as if she owned it. And the look on her face told everybody that she knew it too.

"It's her. It's Distillery Rodbottom. And she's with her husband, Nil Jiffyson."

Wag and Scally both heard the same message. Scally quickly walked forward to get next to his buddy.

"Keep it cool, Wag," he whispered. "We've got to be careful around this one."

Wag nodded. "Yeah, she's the suspicious dynamite here."

"Why don't you try to check out Nil. Remember, *check him out* – you know what we're looking for, right? And I'll try to distract Distillery."

"If that's a plan," sniffed Wag, "then it's about as appetizing as a McDog burger with freedom fries." He moved away with his tray and drinks and began circulating.

The VIDs in the Reception Hall were all dutifully mingling with a cascade of false smiles and arrogance. Wag wished he could wipe the smugness from their faces. But he had a job to do. He was, after all, a trained undercover agent and provocateur – not a street dog with a grudge. And Wag knew very well how to play the part. Wag was well aware of what he was doing. His smile too was false. It was, he thought, very much like being an avatar in some video game. Here we go, he muttered to himself, as he moved closer to Distillery and Nil.

"What champagne is this?" demanded the American Pit Bull Terrier with a snarl. The energy was heavy and unwelcoming. There was a fierce and unfriendly atmosphere around her.

"It's the best champagne that money can buy," answered Wag, improvising quickly.

Distillery grunted. "And what is that?"

"It is a Dom Pérignon Rose," replied Wag, remembering his snobbery training back at Dog Intelligence HQ.

Distillery scratched her snubby nose. "In that case, bring me a Dom Pérignon Rose Gold."

"Certainly." Wag turned away, giving a well-timed smile to Nil to check his reaction. Nil smiled back but his features were expressionless.

"That's funny," Wag whispered as he walked away.

"What is?" asked Tuesday from the other end.

"That Nil guy is an Akita Ken breed. Those breeds always show facial expressions. They speak by expressions more than words. But this dude has a face as sturdy as a judge's spanking stick." Wag moved away to the back of the room. Scally had picked up on the request and, in a flash, he was in the kitchens rummaging through their chilled champagne collection.

"Do we have a Dom Pérignon Rose Gold?"

The head caterer laughed. "You must be kidding me – not on Frumpus's watch. He doesn't even drink alcohol. Not a drop. We have a whole fridge stacked full of diet cola just for him. Here, take this – it's a Chandon California Brut Classic. They won't know the difference, those snob-dogs out there. All fur and no style." Scally opened the bottle and poured several glasses of the California Brut, then hurried back to the room.

Frumpus was prancing about the Reception Hall garnering as much attention as he could. He seemed to be in his element, acting as the Presidog of the United States of Ameridog. He was wagging his head cheerily as Geegee Bushtail, the Beagle, was chatting away. They seemed to be getting on well, each vying to be the last one to pat the other on the back. When Geegee patted, then Frumpus had to pat back – and on it went. Bo-Ma shuffled over trying to squeeze into the camaraderie, but Frumpus wasn't having any of it.

"Hey, Bo-Ma. You were invited here because I had to invite you – but don't try to cuddle up with your peace prize talk. We all know you honey-potted your way into getting that sham prize."

Bo-Ma tried his hardest to show a sad face.

"Don't pretend you're miffed at me," continued Frumpus. "Yes, we can – no, we can. You're just a jalopy running on empty slogans. Now off you trot and enjoy the free food. Oh, sorry old boy, but we haven't got any pizza on the menu."

Bo-Ma pulled an ugly face. Frumpus smiled and turned back to Geegee Bushtail.

"You're getting close to the wire, old friend," said Geegee.

Frumpus shrugged. "Someone has to, sooner or later. The shenanigans in this town have to stop some time. And you well know who's first in line." Frumpus nodded over in the direction of Distillery who was about to grab another drink.

Distillery looked at Scally with a squinted eye. "Are you sure it's Dom Pérignon Rose Gold?"

"Oh, for sure, Madam. On the word of my dying aunt."

Distillery sniffed and grabbed two glasses. She drank them both in an instant and licked her lips. "Lovely stuff." She burped and moved away with Nil silently following her.

"Don't tell me you have a dying aunt?" asked Thursday in his ear.

"No. Just a dead aunt who died ten years ago trying to bungee jump from Big Ben."

"Nice one."

The ceremonial gong was banged, dinner was announced, and the guests started to move towards the dining room. All the catering staff rushed back to the kitchens to prepare for serving the first course of the evening's menu. Wag and Scally had their targets in sight. Scally was a little hesitant. There was a dangerous aura around Distillery, and it was unnerving. Thursday joked in his ear that maybe she had been drinking young lamb's blood every day to make her strong. Yet right now, lucky for them, they had to focus on her husband, Nil. They needed to find out if the inside rumors were true – was he a clone of her dead husband? Scally had positioned himself to front of house and had just served the first course to Distillery. Wag was attempting to subtly sniff around Nil. The odd thing was, this Nil guy kept smiling as Wag took a quick sniff at his ear.

"Mmm, yes. This looks delicious. What is it?" Nil's expressionless face looked directly at Wag.

"It's creamed puree of smoked eggplant," said Wag, honestly.

"Yes, eggplant. That's good. It reminds me of Haiti," replied Nil.

"Don't be so ridiculous!" snapped Distillery, hearing her husband's remark. "I told you to behave yourself – did I not?" Nil nodded obligingly.

"Eggplant puree, really! That's just so Frumpus – just so *mundane*." Distillery almost spat out the last word as if the very mundaneness of speaking it made her feel ill.

"Ah, but it is a magic eggplant," replied Wag, who could not resist.

"And what's so magic about it?"

"It's an eggplant that has no eggs in it." Wag smiled as he moved away.

"Apologies, Madam," said Scally quickly cutting in. "You'll need to excuse my colleague, he's a few watts low in his lightbulb."

Distillery snorted. "Someone should get him connected to an Alexa lightbulb then. That girl's far smarter."

Wag stayed out of sight but continued watching Nil keenly, waiting for an opportunity. It didn't take too long to come. It was between the puree starter and the second course that Nil stood up and made his way in the direction of the men's room.

"I'm going in," said Wag into his microphone.

By the time he had entered the men's washroom, he saw Nil bending over the wash basin and brushing his teeth. Wag shook his head. No one brushed their teeth between meals in United Kingdog. Wag trotted over and started to wash his hands, waiting for the other guest in the restroom to leave. When it was just the two of them, Wag picked up a White House embroidered towel to dry his hands. He let it slip to the floor.

"Dear me, what slippery paws I have!" Wag went down on all fours as if to get the towel. Instead, he inched over behind where Nil was standing and, screwing up his face, stretched forward to take a sniff. Nothing. There was no glandular smell. But Wag needed to make sure. He stretched further to get a good, deep sniff. But this time he stretched too far, and his damp nose made butthole contact.

"Ahhh, what the holy pups-nuts are you doing!?!"

"Cool it man, I'm just butt-surfing you. It's a VID thing, right?" Wag was trying to improvise.

"Security! Security!" yelled Nil. It was the most animated Wag had seen him all evening.

"Get out of there, now!" screamed Tuesday's voice in his ear. Wag didn't need an executive order. He sprinted out of the men's room and made a dash for the kitchen.

"He's a clone, Tuesday. He's anal glandless."

"Make for the exit. We'll speak later."

But Wag never made it that far. He only managed to get to the pantry door before a large thud landed on him. He was pinned to the ground with a heavy weight on his neck.

"I can't breathe, Man. I can't breathe," were the last things Wag remembered saying.

CHAPTER TEN

Dogs Lives Matter

Tuesday was looking grave. In fact, you could say that she was looking graver than a gravestone. She was also very annoyed. She was annoyed with Wag for getting caught and annoyed with the world for everything else. Scally was somewhat perplexed and trying to figure out what to do next, besides keeping Thursday calm over her sister's annoyance. And then there was Frumpus. Yet not too much was going on there. Frumpus was still trying to figure out which day of the week it was and whether he had any upcoming engagements he didn't know about. And then the phone rang.

The call was put through to Frumpus. It was of Presidog importance, apparently. Frumpus listened at the end of the line for a few minutes, his face dropping lower and lower until his chin was almost drinking his diet cola.

"Oh, come on love…no, no…I'm not dis-loving you, I mean, come on my sweetie…no, no, I'm not sweeting you babe…of course I was loving you before but now that…yes, of course I understand the gravity of the situation but let's not mix affairs here…there are swings and roundabouts, you know that…no, it's not about swinging either….what? No, let's leave Sueme out of this – you can sue me over something else. What about the time I threw your steak out of the window, only that I missed, and the steak stuck to the wall - remember that? Or was the window not open and the steak stuck to the window? I can't remember now. Anyhow, isn't that food harassment – can't you sue me over that? C'mon, why drag Sueme into this – she's just an innocent pussycat…."

Frumpus jerked the phone receiver away from his ear as distant screams could be heard. Then he started to make whooshing noises and blowing through his paws.

"Sorry, cannot hear you," Frumpus shouted into the phone, "the Marine One helicopter has just landed outside my window. I've got to go now – top secret Presidog duties. Speak later…chou chou…" Frumpus slammed down the phone receiver and slumped back into his chair.

"Sir?" Spencer, the Vice Presidog was looking concerned.

"Oh, it's nothing," replied Frumpus with

a casual wave of his paw. "It was just my ex-wife, Ayewanna. She heard about my dilly-dallying with that lady compatriot friend of mine, Sueme."

Spencer nodded his head. "Uh-huh. So, your ex-wife knows about your affair with the Siamese cat, Sueme? Who doesn't know, Sir? With respect, someone leaked the whole affair to the press."

"Exactly!" Frumpus banged his paw on the table. "Some devilish do-daddy leaked my private affairs and now I have to be the one to pay for this?"

Spencer frowned. Although no one was sure whether it was a frown of sympathy or one of *how pathetic*. "And what does Ayewanna want, Sir – if I may ask?"

"Oh, the usual – what else? That Cesky Fousek hound is trying to squeeze my pips for more money. And she's already got more bags of money than a ragged band of bandit leprechauns. Oh well, I guess I better build another tall building somewhere, or sell off one of my golf courses. Hey – what if I sell only the holes on my golf course but keep the grassy areas. Would that work?"

"Sir, with all due respect, we may need to leave this delicate issue for another time. We really do have more immediate concerns to deal with here." Spencer was trying hard to be as diplomatic as possible.

"Do we?"

Scally coughed. "Ahem. Mr Presidog. We

have a national crisis on our paws. We believe we know who may be behind the cloning scam, although we don't yet know why. And there are greater forces at work all over the place that we may never know about. Many of these forces are, no doubt, deep behind this government, as they may be behind many governments." Scally was thinking about his recent trip to the dark side of the moon. Yet he thought it best to return to that subject another time. Frumpus was only good for one biscuit at a time. "And one of our agents is anaesthetized."

A blank look appeared on Frumpus's face. "Annie's tied? Yes, I'm sure she is. And so are my paws. But what's that got to do with the price of sugar?"

"One of our agents is unconscious," said Tuesday in a more forceful tone.

"Really? Who?" Frumpus looked surprise as he scanned the room.

"Agent Wag," said Scally.

Frumpus scratched his belly. "Wag…Wag… you say?"

"My partner," said Scally, irritably.

"Ah yes, yes, that scruffy fella who talks in a muffled tone like he's chewing on something at the same time. So, first dog first. Who's behind this cloning business? Who's trying to infiltrate this fantastic Cabinet of mine? Who would dare?"

Frumpus slurped from his diet cola as he listened to Scally give his version of the story. Vice Presidog Spencer listened, looking increasingly concerned.

Spencer coughed into his large paw. "Ahem, well, regarding Agent Wag, I feel confident we can expect a full recovery. Nil Jiffyson's agents gave a good dose of a powerful smelling agent to knock him out. He'll be shaky when he comes around, but he'll be okay. We use that stuff ourselves for grabbing dangerous mutts."

"If he's just a little shaky then he'll more or less be his normal self." Scally tried to smile, but he was concerned over his buddy.

"Distillery Rodbottom has her paws all over this," added Thursday. "She's the brute that's really calling the shots."

Spencer nodded. "Indeed. And if she's really in charge of all this like you agents suspect, then she'll be wanting to move things ahead. She may even think that we're onto her."

"I've never been onto her," added Frumpus, obviously unaware of the drift of the conversation. "I've never found her attractive. A bit too Hell Houndish for my taste."

It was dark. And Wag was thirsty. And…and…… am I lying in a four-poster bed? he thought. This is a real bummer. Four-poster beds are for aristo nuts, or molly-coddled Chihuahuas. Either way, this Wag has got to get his pooch-ass out of here. Wag struggled to pull the sheets away from him and realized just how weak he really was. Bugger! He fell off the high bed with a large thud. Crappy smellhole Wag, can't you even stand up? Wag was talking to himself and although he could hear the words perfectly in his head they seemed to come out like a slurred warble.

Whilst Wag was fiddling with his tongue, trying to straighten it out with his paws, another meeting was going on in an office deep within the halls of Congress...

Distillery Rodbottom picked a tooth with her pointed toenail. She was trying to get out a scrap of lizard meat that had been lodged in there since breakfast.

"There – got it!" She gulped it down and licked her lips. "Right, where were we?"

The room was a smart-looking office that clearly belonged to a person of high ranking. All the furniture was lush and no doubt expensive. It was the best of the best because Distillery was sitting in an office of the Capital Building on Capital Hill. And she was seated in a soft leather armchair speaking with Pansy Ploppy, House Barker of Ameridog Kennel of Representatives. Yet you shouldn't let the name Pansy Ploppy fool you into thinking she was a ploppy, floppy kind of breed. This Pansy was a Dogo Argentino breed and a fierce contender beside Distillery. Together, they appeared as a formidable pair. A pair of pouncers – not pooches.

Distillery looked hard into the face of her old pal. "Things are going too slow, Pansy. We need to get the program moving faster. We need to get Frumpus out of office. An office that he should never have had in the first place. It wasn't *for him*." She gritted her teeth in anger.

Pansy stared back hard and nodded. "Too right, Distillery. That popularist geek got handed a lucky ticket. He's a nuisance to our plans and, more than that, he's insufferable. He makes Geegee Bushtail look like a virgin saint."

Distillery smiled one of her rare Pit Bull smiles. "The clones were a great idea, but we didn't consider the time needed for their integration into the Cabinet. They couldn't become operational immediately. And now I suspect that Frumpus, or rather some of the clever ones left around him, may be onto us. At least, they're beginning to smell a dead rat."

"Or Nil's butt," replied Pansy in reference to the White House dinner incident.

Distillery grunted. "That Britdog agent certainly got in our way. Nil is not important to us. It doesn't matter that they know he's a clone. No one will miss the real one – that snivelling Tonica slurper."

This time Distillery showed her full set of teeth. She had a nasty bite to her.

"What do you propose?" Pansy sat back in her swivel chair and sipped on a sparkling tonic water.

"You still putting vodka into those? Anyway, what I propose is activating one of our open society funded operations. It's time for *Dogs Lives Matter* to earn its keep."

"Nice one. That was a real coup setting up that organization. No one suspects a thing. It's the toast of the town. We can literally get away with murder for that."

Distillery grinned. "We may have to."

"Shall I get the team activated?"

"Red alert-X. I want them into formation within three days." Distillery rose from her seat. "Get them battle-suited. We've got a riot on our hands. Now I'm taking a walk." Distillery left the office and trotted down the corridor with her security team following close behind. She wanted to have a look around the halls of Congress. Wouldn't it be just great if we got a riot going on in here, she thought to herself. She felt as if she were queen of Washington D.C. One way or another, she was determined to bring on the downfall of Frumpus. She despised that fool.

"Don't be a fool, Wag. You need to rest a little." Tuesday was trying to get Wag back into the high bed. He was heavier than he looked.

"I'm big-boned, baby," said Wag, trying to keep his tongue out of the way of his words. "Hey, where are all my clothes?" he asked, looking down at himself.

"Someone had to undress you, and it certainly wasn't going to be a dog-in-black." Tuesday smiled at Wag. "Besides, I wanted to see if what they say about Britdog agents is true."

"And is it?"

"True enough, you Wag. Now get some rest or I'll ship you off to the Louisiana State Penitentiary."

Twenty-two minutes later and Wag walked into the briefing room. The rest of the crew were seated around an octagonal table. His partner and buddy, Scally, was there, as were Tuesday, Thursday, Frumpus, Vice Presidog Spencer, and Podenko, the Captain of US Presidog Guards.

"Hope I'm not late – I had a chloroform trip that banged my balls to the burner. Now then, what's the plan, Stan?"

Frumpus looked around the room. "Stan the caterer isn't in here, is he?"

"We're planning to make a raid onto Distillery Rodbottom's ranch," said Podenko. "We need to wait until we know she is there. It's best we take action away from Washington. It's got to be out of the public and media eye. You know, as hush-hush as possible."

"Hushy-wushy-husky," interrupted Frumpus, putting a paw to his lips as if to signal a whisper. "We don't want Distillery getting wind of our arrival. She's enough of a windbag already." Frumpus chuckled at his own joke.

"And Distillery usually retreats to her ranch at the weekend, apparently," added Scally. He was glad to see his buddy back again.

Tuesday gave Wag a dirty look, as if to say: "I told you to stay in bed." Wag gave her a cheeky smile back as if to say: "my face only looks like it can read your mind, but I haven't the slightest inclination."

"It's Monday today, so that gives us five days to prepare," said Podenko.

"To the Bat Cave!" shouted Frumpus.

Distillery entered the building of her charity organization, the *In-Tonic Foundation*. It always made her smile when entering, thinking how the world outside believed that her foundation was doing philanthropic work. Morons, she often repeated to herself. Distillery lived in a black and white world where she believed there were only two classes – the morons and the merciless. And she definitely did not count herself amongst the morons. As far as she was concerned, the vast majority, who made up the moronic class, were sleeping on the day that the Great Dog in the Sky was handing out brains.

Distillery walked past her employees as if they were lamp shades. For her, all these extra bodies were just additional decoration. Maybe once in a while she would have to speak to someone in the building, yet she did it automatically. The thing about Distillery was that she thought everyone else was inferior to her. And she was also convinced that no one had a superiority complex greater than hers. She storm-trooped into her office and slammed the door shut behind her. As usual, her personal security goons had to wait outside. It didn't matter – they were clones too and so she couldn't hurt their feelings, no matter how hard she tried. And in the beginning, she had tried very, very hard indeed. Then she soon tired of it. Distillery opened her private extra-security smartphone and pressed just one button. The phone rang.

"Good day, my dear Presidog." A suave European sounding voice answered at the other end.

"I should be the Presidog, and you know it."

"I've always known it. Now, for what do I owe the pleasure?"

"Just to inform you that we are accelerating our plans. We have an 'Event' planned in three days that will escalate the situation. The Clone Plan is taking too long. The quicker we can get Frumpus off his throne, the quicker we can continue our operations." There was a pause.

"That is good to hear." The other voice was calm, balanced, and not showing any nuance or tone of emotion.

"How are things at your end?" continued Distillery.

"Things are always fine here. We have plans within plans. Our operations with you are only one leg of the spider."

"Well, you can tell the *Council of Nine* that I'm sorting things out here, not to worry." There was an even longer pause.

"I remind you not to speak openly of the council."

Distillery shook her head. "We're on a secure line. No one's messing with my phone."

"I remind you that nothing is secure. I am not concerned about your phone. I am considering the Leonardo satellites. These you do not own. Lastly, you do not need to tell us not to worry. We do not worry. It is only you that should be worrying…if things do not go well." The phone line went dead.

"Infuriating brute," muttered Distillery to herself. Yet secretly she hoped that no surveillance device was listening to her. If *he* ever heard her saying this about him, then they'd be trouble. Even in her own office she could not be one hundred percent sure she was not being surveyed herself. Distillery knew better than most that the world they now lived in was under constant surveillance. Freedom was a word that belonged to the past. Everyone was under suspicion, and everyone could be tracked. It was, she again reminded herself, a world of the morons and the merciless.

She hoped the Dogs Lives Matter plan would work.

Three days later...

Scally was looking through some classified governmental papers that Podenko had delivered to him. Scally wanted to know more about the background of Distillery Rodbottom and her now-cloned husband, Nil Jiffyson. Beside him sat Thursday, being her organized and diligent self. They worked well together, although Scally sensed that some distance had crept into their relationship recently. Thursday seemed, well, a little *off* at times. At first, Scally had put it down to her anxiety about the upcoming plan. But now, he was not so sure.

Wag looked over at Scally and grinned. Ah yes, thought Scally, Wag and me working together, now that's a completely different thing. That's a *dog-buddy thing*. With Thursday, it was a different way of working.

"Do you think Nil Jiffyson is really dead,

or just lying low whilst his clone takes over all his duties?" Thursday looked over at Scally, waiting for a reply.

Scally thought for a bit. "Either way, he's dead inside. Once you give your life to a clone, you lose a part of yourself." Thursday listened to the answer. It seemed to make her withdraw further within. She looked pensive about something. Something, whatever it was, appeared to be in a struggle within her. "Besides," added Scally, "after Nil's affair with Tonica Doginsky, he's probably better off being dead around Distillery." They both laughed at that.

"What's all the fun, aren't you guys working?" asked Tuesday, taking out her earpods and brushing back her Golden Labrador hair. She lay back on the sofa, dressed in her spotted pajamas.

"What you listening to, sweet pajamas?" asked Wag as he strolled into the salon with a mug of tea in his paw.

Tuesday looked up. "Oh, just some of my favorite Dog Dylan."

"Cool. Is that dude still alive? I heard he was sculpturing his own funeral elegy?"

"I think so. Not sure. He's been a recluse for years. He just makes his metal sculptures."

The four agents were back at Tuesday's house. They were waiting it out until the weekend for when the raid on Distillery's ranch had been planned. Podenko,

as Captain of US Presidog Guards, was keeping
them up to date with the planning. Wag sprawled on
the sofa next to Tuesday and tossed his legs over her.

"Hey, Mr. Chloroform, I'm not your leg rest!"

Wag leaned back. "That's right, you're my
everything."

Suddenly, the phone rang and Scally hastily
picked it up. A few seconds later and he slammed it
down.

"Everyone, grab your things. We gotta get
moving – now!"

"What's up?" called out Thursday, scrambling
to her feet.

"Big trouble on Capital Hill. We got a riot on
our hands."

Tuesday swung her '65 Shelby Mustang into the
street and roared away through the traffic. Thursday
was seated beside her and chatting away on her
phone trying to get intel. Wag and Scally were in the
back seat being tossed around from side to side.

"Tuesday can sure drive," stammered Scally,
holding on to the back of the seat in front of him
where Thursday sat.

"Yep. She's a mean speed canine machine,"
replied Wag, slipping down the seat.

A short while later and the car came to a sudden halt.
The road ahead was blocked by a riotous throng of

dogs. Dogs of all sizes, colors, and breeds. They were waving placards with slogans scrawled over them. Many had *Dogs Lives Matter* written on them. Others had slogans such as *Hands Up, Don't Shoot This Dog*, and *This Dog Can't Breathe*, and *Is My Dog Next?*

There was no way to move forward. They had to leave the Mustang, yet again, and try to move along with the throng. There were shouts, chanting, even some dog wailing, all filling the air. The energy was tense and nervous. All four agents could feel it in their dog bones.

"They're heading up to the Capital Building. They're almost there." Tuesday tried to jump up to see over the heads of the crowd. Wag got behind her and lifted her up. "They're at the steps already."

"I don't like the feel of this," said Scally. He could sense that something was in the air.

"Put a bunch of dogs together and feed them a bone, and you have madness," added Wag.

"Exactly," said Scally, frowning. "But what's the bone?"

"Who are those guys on the steps?" asked Tuesday, pointing ahead of them. Sure enough, now that they had edged closer amongst the throng, they saw a group of dogs dressed as activists, yet they had different slogans and their attire looked odd. One of them was holding high a placard with the slogan: **Glutin for Presidog of Ameridog**. Another had one that read: **Frumpus is friend of Rushindogs**.

Wag noticed it first, having the revolutionary eye. He noticed that this particular group of activists were wearing Rushindog symbols on their jackets. He poked Scally, who saw it too.

"They're Rushindog agents?" he asked.

Wag shook his head. "Nah, I doubt it. They don't smell like Rushindogs – or like revolutionaries for that matter."

Then it all clicked. "Ah, they're hired saboteurs," said Scally. "They've been paid to infiltrate the mob. They're here for another reason."

Wag and Scally grabbed Tuesday and Thursday and pulled them to the side. And just in time. The roar of the mob moved forward. Placards were hurled to the ground and trampled upon as the crowd heaved and pushed and moved up the steps of the Capital Building. The group of fake revolutionaries were leading the way. Or rather, they were charging the way forward. And surprisingly, they were finding no resistance. Thursday and Tuesday both noticed the unusual absence of the regular security force. As CIA agents, they were well informed of the armed security around Washington D.C., and especially around the Capital Building where Congress was located.

"This smells off," remarked Thursday. Her sister Tuesday nodded in agreement.

They watched as the first wave of protestors swept over the top steps of the Capital Building without resistance and swarmed into the building itself. There were barks and roars of jubilation and anarchy all mixed into one mad howl.

"I've seen the best minds of my generation destroyed by madness," muttered Wag under his breath.

"Come on," said Scally, "we have to follow them in."

The two CIA and the two Britdog agents merged with the mob as it surged into the Capital Building with an almost blind force. It was mayhem.

CHAPTER ELEVEN

Chaos in Congress

It was pandemonium at first. Crazy, wailing, shrieking activists were storming Congress and running through the main doors shouting stock slogans as if they'd been fed with them beforehand. And yet once inside, all pretense of protest and revolution suddenly ceased. It was as if all the craziness was only for the cameras, as there had been several TV crews outside filming the riot. After the initial mayhem and bedlam, everyone settled down to a more leisurely trot through the interior halls and corridors. Some activists strolled around admiring the works of art as if on a visit to a museum.

"You're not getting paid to view the scenery," said Wag to one small group of protestors. They shook their heads as if they didn't understand. "Bah, amateurs!" Wag waved them off.

They decided to split up. Tuesday and Thursday went in one direction while Wag and Scally went another. It wasn't long before the Brit agents came across a security guard chatting amiably with a few protestors and explaining the meaning of one of the grand pictures hanging on the wall. The guard eyed them both with a suspicious look.

"Are you with the team?" he asked.

"Sure," replied Scally. "Why else would we be here?"

"You don't look like the others, that's all."

"We're deeper operatives, we have other orders," added Wag.

The security guard nodded and smiled. He seemed to know the score. It was soon evident that neither of them was supposed to be there. And this could prove to be dangerous. Perhaps they were expected to have a secret password or sign that identified them as part of the arranged crowd. They had to keep low, not to get singled out or identified. They had to make sure their presence would not seem suspicious.

Scally led Wag into a side office.

"We need to warn the ladies. They need to know they're on enemy territory. This whole thing is a set-up."

"And we're not a part of it."

"Exactly." Scally flipped out his phone and pressed. It rang a few times before Thursday answered.

"Scally, what's up?"

"We all need to get out of here – now! This riot was rigged and we're not on the team. If we get caught in here, we could fall into their paws."

"Yeah, I know. It feels really weird. It's like we've gate-crashed someone's party and we're not on the guest list.'

"Sure thing. Let's meet back at Tuesday's place asap – got it?"

"Okay."

"Be careful, Thurs."

"You too, Scal."

Wag looked over at his buddy. "Thurs?"

"Abbreviation is a form of affection. Come on, Waggamonster."

Scally looked over at the nearby desk. On it was an expensive looking laptop. That could serve our purposes, he thought. Scally grabbed it and led the way out of the office and down a long corridor. Wag followed, not knowing where it was going to take them. Suddenly, from the far end, a group of protestors emerged from one side of the corridor and began walking towards them. When they were up close to one another, several of the protestors eyed

Wag and Scally carefully, unsure of where they each stood.

Scally raised his arm which had the laptop held below. "We're on the tech team. We've got this covered."

"NSA?" asked one of the protestors, who was wearing an antler deer hat on his head.
Scally's brain whirred for a few micro-seconds. Ah, the National Security Agency. He was just about to reply that they were indeed with the NSA when Wag stepped forward and made an odd waggle of his paw in front of the protestors.

"These aren't the droids you're looking for."
The protestors, who all looked youthful, stared back blankly.

"Damn illiterate nerf herders," said Wag as he grabbed the laptop from under Scally's arm and tossed it down the corridor. "Bomb!" he shouted. "It's going to blow!" Wag nudged Scally and they both made a run for it. The group of protestors didn't know what to do. They panicked and then ran off down the other adjacent corridor. After a few seconds they stopped, looked at one another, then abruptly turned around to chase after Wag and Scally.

"What the hairy ass kind of stunt was that?" shouted Scally as they continued running.

"My Jedi mind trick," shouted back Wag.

"And does it work?"

"Only on imbeciles."

After running down a polished wooden staircase they entered a lobby area and spotted a double exit door not far away. Mingling near the exit were one, or perhaps two, film crews. Scally shouted over.

"Hey, the intruders are coming this way." Scally was now walking fast. He approached the film crew and flipped out a police badge that he waved in front of their faces before slipping it back into his waistcoat pocket. He pointed over his shoulder. "They're coming this way. Get their faces on camera and you'll have the best scoop of the year."
The film crews immediately jumped into action, getting their cameras pointed and rolling and blocking the door with their presence. But it didn't matter as by that time Wag and Scally were already outside, trotting down the steps of the Capital Hill building, and quickly submerged within the crowds of bystanders.

"Hey, where did you get your Ameridog police badge from?" asked Wag, as they cruised into a wide avenue in the back of a taxi.

"From the Pop Tarts box in Tuesday's kitchen. It's a toy Brooklyn Nine-Nine badge."

"Slick, dude. Slick."

Later that afternoon they were both watching the television news at Tuesday's place. Tuesday and Thursday had not yet returned and both Wag and

Scally were showing mild concern. On the news was Pansy Ploppy, House Barker of Ameridog Kennel of Representatives, giving a theatrical performance on the Congress riot and blaming it fully on Frumpus. It didn't look good. Ploppy was saying that Rushindog activists had broken into the Capital Hill building after first sabotaging the Dogs Lives Matter peaceful march. Frumpus was at fault, she continued to tell the media, because he had been too soft with Glutin and the Rushindogs. They were literally eating crunchies from the same bowl. Frumpus had incited the riot due to his disrespect for Dogocracy and the rule of law. And finally, declared Pansy Ploppy with all her bullish attitude, there was nothing left to do but to impeach Presidog Frumpus.

"You hear that Scally? The Demodogs want to impeach Frumpus and get the Republicdogs out of the government."
Scally was positioned at the window, keenly eyeing the street. Wag guessed he was worried for Tuesday and Thursday. It was getting late, and they had not yet returned or left a message. Scally dialed his mobile phone again. There was no ringing at the other end. Then some movement caught Scally's eye. A large black vehicle pulled up across the road. Two well-dressed and heavy built dogs got out, surveyed the street carefully, then began walking towards their front door.

"Prepare yourself, Wag – we've got company."

Wag leapt off the sofa and positioned himself behind a pillar, his tazer in hand. There was a knock at the door.

A deep voice called out. "Agent Scally and Agent Wag – we know you are both in there. We're from the Federal Bureau of Investigation. We only wish to talk with you both. We need to take you in for questioning."

"Fed agents?" asked Wag in a low whisper.

"I doubt it. Fed agents don't drive black armored Humvees." Scally peeked out again from behind the window curtain. Something wasn't right, and he felt it instinctively.

"Agents Wag and Scally – we will need to take you in. Open the door or we'll be forced to take other measures," said the deep voice.

Scally knew it was only a matter of time, and they were already short on it. "Show us some ID first," he called back. Scally was trying to stall for time whilst thinking of a plan, or a timely intervention.

"Open the door and we'll show our IDs."

Scally thought again. "What's the reason for needing to speak with us. We are Britdog agents."

There was a pause, and some whispers from the other side of the door. And then finally – "You are to be questioned over complicity to commit foreign interference into domestic affairs."

"Smells like a rat's fart in a pumpkin pie," whispered Wag to his buddy.

"Are you going to open the door?" the voice asked again.

"Yeah, okay. I'll just get the keys. Hold your horses."

Scally beckoned over to Wag to follow him. They crept upstairs and into one of the back bedrooms.

"We're going out the window and over the roof, right?" asked Wag.

"What makes you think that?"

Wag looked at his buddy and smiled. "That's what they always do in the movies," he replied. Scally knew he was right.

"Why don't we just open the door and jump them?"

Scally didn't like this idea. "Because they're built like Confederate statues, and they'll be armed. Everyone's armed over here. We're not prepared to meet them on their terms. We need to meet them on ours."

"Which are?" asked Wag, casually.

"Stealth," Scally replied as he crept out through the open window and onto the slanting roof. Just then there came a large crashing sound as the front door was smashed open. Wag hopped through the window, lost his footing on the tiles, fell onto his back, then rolled down the roof and knocked Scally off his feet. YAAAHHH...both Britdog agents went bouncing off the roof and landed in a grassy, overgrown back lawn. Stealth is for geeks, anyway, thought Wag as he brushed himself down.

"I'm going back in." Wag started walking to the back door of the house. He lifted up the doormat and pulled out a key. "Good job the Feds don't check doormats," he said with a grin and let himself in.

"You got a plan, Wag?"

"Yep. I'm going out through the in door." Wag, with Scally following him, walked through the kitchen, into the hallway, and stepped over the smashed front door and into the street. They could hear that the Feds were still upstairs. The last place they would suspect Wag and Scally to be would be back in the house, Wag had reasoned. They walked down the street swiftly. Yet it would only be a matter of time.

They had only gone a few paces when a black SUV swerved into the street and screeched to a halt beside them. The door opened.

"Get in, boys – quick!"

"Pod!"

Pansy Ploppy lifted a shot glass of clear liquid and knocked it back in one gulp.

"Still drinking tonic water, Pansy?" Distillery looked over from the desk where she was sitting, tapping away on her laptop. "I hear your laptop was stolen, and then thrown as a fake bomb. At least those Britdog agents have imagination." She looked up over her thick-rimmed spectacles. It was a look of ridicule and disdain mixed together.

"You're seeing double-vision," replied Pansy in a sarcastic tone. "The laptop was not stolen. It was, err, merely coincidentally used as a decoy."

"Be that as it may, Pansy dear, the *Council of Nine* do not like coincidences." Distillery smirked. Pansy winced.

"I want a full-on frontal political assault on Frumpus," continued Distillery. "We need to create our Rushindog Gate moment to take him down. He's starting to snoop too much into our own affairs. We need to keep his nose as far away from our smuggling ring as possible. I don't need to say any more on that!"

Pansy nodded, then knocked back another shot of clear liquid. Her face suddenly appeared to gleam more youthful behind her flattened wrinkles. "I can feel the adrenaline," she said, licking her lips. "Of course, of course. That idiot Frumpus thinks this is just about infiltrating his government and trying to start a war with the Rushindogs. Ha – how short-sighted! For now, he knows nothing about our international smuggling networks…"

"And let's keep it that way," interrupted Distillery.

"And the black operations? The space satellite communications?"

Distillery chewed on her lips as if thinking.

"I suspect some military commanders are loyal to the Presidog. But we still have the upper paw. Frumpus either knows more than he thinks he does or less than he thinks he does. One thing is sure, he doesn't know what he thinks he does."

"Reassuring," replied Pansy.

Meanwhile, the black SUV had driven through an unmarked double-doored garage and into what looked like a run-down warehouse building. Captain Podenko and another, a non-uniformed soldier, led Wag and Scally up a security elevator, through a heavily secured, double-whammy thick door, and into a well-equipped apartment. Inside, a top military commander was waiting for them.

"This is a safehouse," said Podenko. "General Errol and his boys will protect you here."
Scally noticed immediately the state-of-the-art surveillance electronics that protected the place. Wag noticed immediately that the restroom had state-of-the-art Dyson paw-dryers.

"Nice safehouse," said Scally, checking the place out.

"Never a wet paw in this place," added Wag, with a nod of appreciation.

"It's a QA safehouse, and General Errol is a decorated 5-star General. He currently heads the QA operation."

Scally smiled. "Impressive. QA does exist, after all."

"Of course," replied Podenko. "It has a mandate to protect the true sovereignty of the United States of Ameridog. Presidog Frumpus is not aware of our presence, yet we have protected him from day one. If it wasn't for QA, the Presidog would have been assassinated by now. We are preserving our national sovereignty against the deep forces of evil."

"Deep forces of evil?" interrupted Wag. "Sounds demonic. It's like capitalism, aristocracy, and elitism all rolled into one, with a Beyonce soundtrack on the side."

"More evil than the media will ever tell you," said Podenko, looking sad. "There are forces in this world that make the industrial-military-intelligence complex look like bubble-gum."

"No more Tutti Frutti flavor then?"

Podenko gave Wag a penetrating look. "We're well past Tutti Frutti now. I'll let General Errol fill you in a little on QA matters while I head back to the White House. I need to brief Presidog Frumpus on his impeachment. Things are getting hot and hairy at the White House. I'll be back shortly to go deeper with you boys. Welcome to the winning side." Captain Podenko saluted and left.

Scally scanned the apartment. It was dark yet illuminated by a soft light. The windows had been tinted so that they could look outside but no one could see inside. Sensors were placed on all windows, doors, and ceilings. No doubt it was regularly checked for listening bugs. In each room was also placed a small antenna with lights. Wag tried to fiddle with one to see if he could sabotage it.

"I wouldn't do that," said General Errol. "They are electromagnetic radiation detectors. They will flash when they detect we are being attacked by EM waves. We don't want another Havana Syndrome here. Anyway, we need to talk." General Errol was a Boxer breed, a strong dog with a loyal nature and a natural suspicion of strangers.

Wag and Scally made themselves comfortable in the main salon of the safe house whilst General Errol filled them in. It seemed that QA had been tracking the operations of a Deep State group ever since the assassination of Presidog Kennedy's stand-in. Kennedy *may* still be alive, yet that information was above Wag and Scally's pay grade. Then again, using that scale, almost everything was above their pitiful pay grade. Ever since Dogexit, inflation had gone on a fast uphill roller coaster ride in the United Kingdog.

General Errol continued to explain how this Deep State group was connected to a highly secretive elite network that had infiltrated most governments of the western world. And it also ran a highly secretive, and profitable, puppy smuggling ring. At this moment, the puppy smuggling was concentrated on the United States of Ameridog, although its main center of operations was in Europe. QA suspected that the major hubs of this network were based in three locations that had special legal protection: the City of London; the Vatican City; and Washington D.C.

"Jeeezz, they're the same places that have their bases on the dark side of the moon," said Scally.

General Errol agreed. "Yes, we are aware of that. That's why we placed one of our operatives, Commander Thursday Adams, into the US Lunar Base operations to infiltrate this network."

"And??" said Scally eagerly. He wanted to hear news about Thursday.

"We started getting good intel from Commander Adams. Then communications ceased for a while. The last information we got from her didn't turn out to be…well, quite so useful. We are concerned for her, especially since the Deep State uses a lot of mind programming methods."

"We need to find her immediately then!" Scally was also feeling concerned for his friend Thursday.

"And Tuesday too," added Wag.

General Errol nodded in agreement. "This elite network moves fast. They tend to always be one step ahead of us. We suspect that many of our own military units have been compromised. And yours too, in Great Britdog. You guys need to be careful now that you know this stuff. Just having this information can get you killed."

"But do they know that *we* know?" asked Wag.

"They know you know something because they know you were on the moon base. By the way, what the darn hell were you guys doing up there in the first place?"

"Thursday took us up there," added Scally.

"Why would she compromise you like that?" General Errol frowned but he didn't have an answer. And neither did Wag or Scally.

The safe house was silent and dark that night. Scally went to this room. Something was on his mind, and he needed to be alone to think. Wag sat on the sofa drinking mugs of tea and reading some magazines that had been left in the house. They were mostly June's Military Intelligence magazines, although Wag had no idea what June knew about military intelligence. General Errol stayed at the safe house with one of his officers. Wag wished he could be alone, especially since he liked to spend a lot of time in the bathroom doing his stuff without strangers listening. But, well, circumstances had changed, and an experienced agent like Wag had no problem adapting his expulsion routines. Nothing much else happened that first night. Scally didn't leave his room. And Wag had an odd nightmare about a gang of midget dogs dressed as clowns chasing Wag through a run-down funfair. When Wag awoke, he needed an extra strong coffee with scrambled eggs and chilies. There were no chilies in the house. Wag was furious. He went straight to the bathroom and made the walls vibrate.

Wag came out of the bathroom pleased with how the Dyson paw-dryer had dried his paws in a matter of seconds. Captain Podenko was in the main room speaking excitedly with General Errol. Scally had recently joined them.

"Wag, come listen to this," said Scally as he waved his buddy over.

Wag trotted over and listened as Podenko informed them that the Canine Intelligence Agency had picked up a private signal transmitted from Commander Thursday's location chip.

"Location chip? What do you mean – she's tagged?"

Podenko looked at Wag and Scally and nodded. "Yes, she agreed to have an implant embedded in her body. It always emits a weak signal, so it cannot be detected by the usual devices. It's on our wavelength, and we know where she is."

"Great!" Scally looked genuinely pleased. "We're going in. You've got a task force prepared, right?"

"We sure do. Ready to roll and rumble," replied Podenko. He was also keen to get some plan into action and to make a first strike against the enemy.

"Cool with me," added Wag. "Where there's a Thursday there's going to be a Tuesday. Where is the location?"

"A pizza restaurant in downtown Washington D.C."

"They're having pizza?"

CHAPTER TWELVE

Pizza Take out

Pansy Ploppy was feeling very pleased with herself. So pleased in fact that she decided to treat herself to a take-out pizza. She asked her assistant to order a thick-base, medium sized Hawaiian pizza. Of course, as any half-decent pizza-eater knows, a pizza with pineapple topping is just not a real pizza – not by a long stretch. But Pansy was one of those dogs that thought they were a leader when in fact they were a follower and a servant of others. Pansy lived in self-denial about this, which is why the high office of politics suited her perfectly. She waited eagerly for her pizza fix whilst sorting through the impeachment papers. The Demodogs had worked overtime to get the papers put together. Pansy was happy with the way things were going. She rubbed her paws together. Things were so much juicier when laced with a dollop of evil, she thought. She growled and bared her strong Dogo Argentino teeth, just for fun. Pansy enjoyed it when she appeared menacing. And she was right to think that Frumpus was feeling nervous.

Vice Presidog Spencer trotted into the Oval Office with a wad of papers clutched in his paws.

"We're going to overturn this, Presidog, Sir. Pansy Ploppy may think she's got the cat in the bag, but we've got the bull by the horns."

Frumpus sipped anxiously on his diet cola through a straw. "Spencer, cut it out with all those animal idioms, metaphors, memes, or whatever they are – they really get my goat. I advise you to look this horse in the eye and give it to me straight. I can handle it, I'm not pig-headed. Those Demodogs are on a wild goose chase but I'm not going to let them weasel out of this one. I've been watching Pansy Ploppy like a hawk and to me she's always seemed like a fish out of water. And that damn Distillery Rodbottom is as mad as a hornet. This impeachment is all a red herring. Don't they know that good ole Ameridog Frumpus wouldn't hurt a fly?"

Spencer tried not to flinch. He stood as sturdy as an elephant. "We have an impeachment hearing coming up. We'll need to do some practice runs. I've asked a speech consultant to come over shortly."

Frumpus banged on the desk and a mop of Poodle white hair flopped over his face. He brushed it back with a licked paw. "I don't never need no speech consultant. I'm part of the Frumpus clan. And the Frumpus clan ain't no never needed a speech nerd to tell us what we need to know. Pay him off or shoot him!"

"It's a *her*, Sir."

"Ah, well, why didn't you say so? You'd better show her in then." Frumpus breathed into his paw and smelt it.

Back at the safe house everyone was getting prepared for the raid. Within an hour or so the armed military would be arriving, and then they'd be on the road. Podenko was taking no chances. He wanted a fully trained and armed squad to go in, pizza restaurant or not. Scally was looking a little preoccupied. He kept checking his phone as if expecting something to come in. Something did, yet from the look on his face it was obvious it was not what he was expecting.

"Shizer, its *W*. She wants a video call with us – now!"

Wag looked over from the sofa. "Crap muffins! What, now?"

W's pug face was not looking so smug. It was, if truth be told, practically steaming. The head of Dog

Intelligence was glaring into the video screen. Wag had been wise to leave all the official talking to Scally, as always.

"What the crittering hell have you guys been up to?"

Scally kept his cool. "Only doing all things necessary to keep on the case."

"And where is your case located?"

"In the United States of Ameridog, ma'am," replied Scally, not one hundred percent sure where this was going.

"Then tell me what in the name of Humping Hercules were you doing on the moon?!" *W*'s face had contracted into a spiral of distorted flesh wrinkles.

"Ah, the moon. Yes, that was an unexpected diversion. Yet it turned out to be integral to our investigation."

"How so?"

Scally paused. He was uncertain of how much information to give out at this time, especially since a highly secretive element in the City of London were involved. Did *W* know of this? Could she be trusted?

"And just how did you come to know about our moon visit?" he asked cautiously.

W breathed in and out heavily several times. "I've had some big wigs from upstairs breathing down my neck. Some bodies high up – and I mean *really* high up – have come to learn of your moon visit. And I've been told to pull you off the case – with immediate effect!"

Scally smelt a dead ferret. This went beyond governmental. Maybe this was what General Errol had been talking of. Scally looked *W* in the eyes. "How long have we known each other?"

W pulled a face. "Too long. Longer than your mother's tail, and a bit more."

"And do you trust me? I mean, trust us?" Scally looked aside to Wag who appeared to have faded out mentally into his own world. Still, his body was present, and that was enough.

W chewed on her fleshy lip. "Yeah, I do. That's what worries me. You've obviously stepped on some big paw toes. Bigger than I can chew."

"Can you hold them off for a while?"

"Like we never had this conversation?" *W* gave her smug pug smile.

"Exactly. Say you couldn't get hold of us. We were in the middle of a raid – which we shortly will be."

"Okay. I got your back on this one. But be careful you two, there are elements out there that are beyond Dog Intelligence. I can't always protect you."

"Thanks *W* – I got you. Oh, and one last thing. Do me a favor and run a quiet background check on two US CIA agents. They are Commander Thursday Adams and her sister, Tuesday Adams." Scally signed off and put his phone away.

"Something on your mind?" Wag glanced over at his partner.

"Suspicions, old buddy. Just suspicions, as always," replied Scally.

The armored vehicles were on the move. In one vehicle were Wag, Scally, Captain Podenko, and several high-ranking military officers. General Errol and his men were in another. Podenko could read Scally's inquisitive face.

"Yes," said Podenko with a curt glance over at the Britdog agents. "These men are loyal to the QA organization. We can't trust the D.C military police on this one. Those dudes are all under the jurisdiction of the state governor. And most governors are in the pockets of the Deep State."

How deep does this deep thing go, wondered Wag as he sat back and fiddled with his bulletproof armored jacket. It was so constraining. He had an itch under his third nipple and needed so badly to scratch it. He was going to ask Scally how his nipples were but noticed he was busy checking his newly issued Beretta M9 pistol. Wag didn't really go in for the US toys. He preferred to keep his own equipment, especially his ninja throwing blades. Wag was more of an up close and personal type of combat guy. And yes, he loved his tazer too - it was a new favorite in his arsenal.

"I've always found warfare so physically lazy," muttered Wag to his companion.

"The art of war, as laid out by Sun Tzu, is truly a dying art," agreed Scally.

"The supreme art of war is to subdue the enemy without fighting," replied Wag, quoting directly from Sun Tzu.

"Supreme excellence consists of breaking the enemy's resistance without fighting," said Scally, also quoting Sun Tzu.

"Win your war before going to war, then you have more time for a personal massage," said Wag with a smile.

Scally thought for a moment. "Was that Sun Tzu?"

"Nope. My very fav philosopher, the wise Lo-Poo."

The vehicles came to a sudden halt. The doors opened and everyone jumped out. Across and further down the street lay their target – Asteroid Pizzeria. Plastered upon its frontage were several signs on which were written: 'Temporary Closure for Renovation.'

"How convenient," said Podenko with a grunt.

"How inconvenient," muttered Wag, "no bonus pizza."

The Britdog agents were told to stay back as the

armed special forces moved toward their target. The street was eerily quiet. It was a downtown area but not central, and away from the main avenues. The few civilian dogs who had been nearby had scampered away fast when they saw the armored vehicles approach. Now the whole area was sealed off. General Errol was in charge of the operation, and he was taking no chances. There was a possibility they would find nothing at the pizzeria. Still, precautions always had to be taken; especially when dealing with such slippery enemies.

Scally was quietly hoping that Thursday and Tuesday would be found safe and well inside Asteroid Pizzeria. The only thing he could be sure of was that he could be sure of nothing. Wag was also secretly hoping that the sisters would be found without incident. He wanted to be served another humdinger delicious breakfast by Tuesday.

General Errol sent in the special forces to raid the Asteroid Pizzeria. He and Podenko took up a command position and watched as they burst down the door of the pizzeria with a battering ram. One after another they entered the building. Scally followed and edged closer, wanting to get a sense of what was going on. Wag had disappeared. He wasn't going to hang around counting his paw nails. He went off to find where the back entrance was. Almost immediately, an explosion erupted from inside the restaurant building. Scally scarpered inside and dive-rolled under the nearest table. A thick smoke had eliminated all visibility. Then another explosion ripped through the building causing more smoke and debris to fall. A large ringing echoed in Scally's ears, blocking out all other sounds. He stayed crouched under the table, unable to move, with eyes squeezed tight to protect from the dust and his paws clamped over his ears to dampen the noise. It was obviously not safe to stay there without moving, and without knowing what was going on. Were they under attack? Scally opened his eyes slightly to try to get some bearings and to see what was going on. After a short while, the haze of dust and smoke began to lift. Scally crawled out from under the table and cautiously moved forward. Luckily for him, he had been the last one to enter the building and so furthest away from the blast radius. All of the special forces were wearing protective gear. Still, no one was expecting an explosion. Scally crawled further ahead of him until he came across several bodies lying on the floor. The guys were wounded. They needed to be taken out of there. Scally grabbed a micro-transmitter from one of the wounded officers. He could hear the voice of General Errol calling to his soldiers.

"We need to get them out of here," replied Scally, coughing with the dust.
Scally could hear moans and shouts coming from further inside. He could also feel movement on the

ground. Then he felt heavy steps behind him as someone landed a large paw upon his shoulder.

"Are you okay? What in the name of Dog is going on here?" It was Captain Podenko. "General Errol is calling in reinforcements. This is a bigger operation than we thought."

"It seems this place was rigged," replied Scally, still coughing.

The inside of Asteroid Pizzeria looked like a bomb zone out of some war movie. Or perhaps it looked more like one of the cities bombed to smithereens by the US war machine. Podenko was checking on all the wounded officers and, with the help of General Errol who was now on the scene, they were evacuating as many officers as they could. One or two who had been at the front were badly injured, with missing limbs. Scally felt disgust. He could never understand how the world of intelligent beings could treat one another like the worst of dogs. It was as if they had no conscience – no empathy or remorse. Maybe those who planned such things were themselves clones? More and more of us are turning into clones, machine-like automatons, thought Scally sadly. It didn't bode well for the future. He stepped forward slowly. It was no time for turning back. They had come here for a reason, after all – a very good reason.

Meanwhile, Wag had been exploring Asteroid Pizzeria from the reverse angle – from the back side. He had managed to crack open a window at the back and climb through when the first of the explosions went off. He had immediately swung into ultra-high Wag alert mode. This Wagamonster was not going to get his testicles blown up, he reasoned to himself. He kept good cover as the next couple of explosions rocked through the building. Parts of the ceiling timber was falling down, making movement about the place dangerous. As soon as he felt it good to move, he crept forward slowly. His eyes were sharp. He didn't want to be on the receiving end of the next hail of nails.

Then he spotted something. Through the dust it had become more visible. It was a thin thread of red light, stretching low across the floor. He didn't move. He stayed still, examining his possibilities. He listened attentively to the sounds coming from the other side of the building. Bodies were being moved around. Yet Wag stayed in his post, as if waiting for an enemy.

A small body in the haze came into view. Wag immediately recognized the contours he knew so well. Not an enemy but a friend.

"Stop where you are. Don't make another step!" called out Wag.

"Wag, is that you?"

"Who else speaks like Wag but Wag. Did your

brains get sizzled?"

Scally was happy to hear the pleasantries of his best buddy.

"There's a trip beam in front of you. A few more steps and you would have been mincemeat for the Asian market."

Scally got down low and scanned the area just ahead. He saw it too. A thin red beam an inch or so above the floor that ran across an arched entrance.

"See any more?"

"Not from here."

"I'm coming over then."

Wag shook his head. Did Scally really need to start hop, skipping, and jumping over laser trip beams when the place was obviously rigged with bombs just waiting to blow flesh bodies to smithereens? Well, the answer was obviously yes because a few seconds later Scally was in front of him.

"Any sign of the girls? Thursday? Tuesday?" Wag shook his head.

Scally took out the micro-transmitter he had kept and sent a message back to Podenko about the laser trip beams. Then he indicated for Wag to follow him as he moved to explore more of the building. At every step, Scally picked up some of the fine dust from the floor and threw it in front of him. Both he and Wag kept their eyes super-sharp for any more bomb tripping devices.

Scally felt the tap on his shoulder as soon as he spotted it too. Ahead of them was a flight of steps leading down. Scally picked up another handful of dust and threw it towards the stairs. Across the top step another thin laser beam could be seen within the dust haze.

Scally turned back to Wag. "If you trip on this beam, I'll kill you."

"If I trip on this beam, I'll kill us both," replied Wag with a wide reassuring smile.

Scally stepped carefully over the beam, making sure the hair on his thin terrier legs kept well away from the laser. He threw some more dust in front of him. The steps leading down appeared to be clean. He took a few steps more to make some space for Wag to follow. Now, the thing you need to know about Wag is that he is a stocky fellow, and he has unusually short legs. His stocky build and stubby legs, which were a remnant from his mixed-blood background, made him sturdy, strong, and almost impermeable to most types of assault (as well as most types of food poisoning). But still, it meant that he was low to the ground. A low step for someone else generally meant a high step for Wag.

Wag hesitated at the top of the steps. He was considering his options.

"Is it all clear down there?" he asked.

Scally nodded. "No more beams on these stairs. It's clear all the way down."

Good, thought Wag. That made it easier to go for Plan B.

"Are you coming or staying?" shouted Scally as he made another step downwards.

Oh, shag-a-rabbit – here goes. Wag took a step back and then leapt from the top of the stairs and landed midway down, hitting Scally and causing them both to roll and bash until they landed with a squat punch on the floor below.

Wag shook the dust off himself and checked if his head was still on the right way round. "I decided to jump." Wag sometimes had a knack for stating the obvious. Scally just preferred it if Wag could state the obvious before the obvious occurred.

"No broken bones," said Scally, although his shoulder stung like doggish hell.

"Sshh," said Wag, putting a paw to his lips for silence. He thought he could hear some muffled sounds. The basement, or wherever they were, was pitch dark. But Scally, being the dog scout that he was, pulled out a flashlight. He was prepared for most things, except Wag's untimely jumps. He shone the beam around the lower room. Over in the corner was a figure of something, or someone. They moved closer. Scally squinted. Wag recognized first who it was.

"That's Nil Jiffyson, Distillery's husband,"

said Wag, remembering how only a short time ago he had been caught sniffing his butt in the White House toilet. Nil was muffled with a tape around his mouth, and he was tied to a wooden chair.

"Wait!" said Scally, grabbing Wag by the arm. "Look what's around his waist." Scally shone the flashlight and they both saw that a bomb belt had been strapped to him.

They were in a dilemma. Should they stay and try to save him – or should they get out fast and save themselves?

It was Wag who said the obvious first. "How do we know if this is just the clone Nil and not the real Nil? If it's the cloned one, then why should we risk our lives to save it?" Wag had a point.

"On the other hand, this could be the real Nil, and this is Distillery's way of getting rid of him for real," replied Scally, thinking it over.

"And I suppose that if we take the tape off his mouth, he'll say he's the real one whether he is or not."

"Exactly," agreed Scally. "Because the clone wouldn't know it's a clone and would say he's real." They both looked at each other, wondering what to do about it.

Scally shrugged, and his shoulder hurt. "You know there's only one way to really find out."

Wag pointed at the tied-up Nil who was

obviously in a great deal of distress. Of course, who wouldn't be, having a bomb belt tied around their waist?

"You think I'm going to try to smell his butt? For one thing, he's tied to a chair. And we can't get him off the chair without the risk of the bomb going off. And maybe it's going to go off anyway? And secondly, do I want to go to doggy heaven from sniffing the butt of a bomb-vested politician, clone or not?" Wag did have a very good point.

The dilemma had turned into a double whammy. If they couldn't know for sure whether the Nil that was tied up was the real one or the clone, then the question now was – do clones represent a real life? Are clones worth risking a life to save?

Scally looked at the poor figure. Only a short while before he had been a top politician strutting his stuff in public and at the White House dinner. And now, he was a sorry looking figure scared to pieces. And whoever left him here thought that his life was worth less than beans. How the once mighty can quickly fall.

"Hold on, Nil, we need to figure something out," said Scally, who by now was starting to feel sorry for the guy. After all, he had always been a pawn in a much bigger game. Nil Jiffyson had been only a stooge with a delusional fantasy of power. At least in Wag and Scally's world, things didn't lose perspective.

The Britdog agents both breathed a deep sigh of relief. They were back on the street outside and away from the dust-filled rubble of the Asteroid Pizzeria. Scally had radioed to Podenko to call in the bomb squad. Both he and Wag had waited until they arrived, trying to reassure Nil that once this was over, it would be good to choose his friends more wisely – and also for him to confess everything. Nil had nodded enthusiastically. They were now hoping that they could learn much more about Distillery's operations from Nil, the insider.

"Good job, boys," said General Errol as they placed Nil into one of the armored vehicles. The bomb squad had managed to disable the nasty flesh-splintering bomb belt. "We're going to take him to headquarters now, and I'm personally going to be questioning him on the way." General Errol saluted and got into the vehicle with Nil.

Wag and Scally, as before, rode along with Captain Podenko and a couple of his officers. The armored vehicle roared into life and pulled away. Wag could see that his friend Scally was feeling saddened inside. It was, he was sure, because they had not found either Thursday or Tuesday. They had searched the rest of what was left of Asteroid Pizzeria, and yet no one else was found. And for this very same reason, Wag was also feeling twisted inside. He was missing his favorite day of the week.

Suddenly, the whole vehicle shook and rocked with a loud bang, then swerved to an abrupt halt. A loud ringing was in everyone's ears.

CHAPTER THIRTEEN

The Raid at Edgewater Ranch

The bomb had killed everyone in the vehicle instantly. General Errol and some of his best officers. This had been a blow to the core of the QA organization. Nil had died too, of course. They only realized later that not only had he been a clone, but that he had been implanted with a particular deadly short-range explosive device. Most likely the clone Nil had been unaware of this.

Captain Podenko was both furious and devastated. He was furious that such an enemy could stoop so low as to create clones as walking bombs. And devastated that he had lost his comrades.

Immediately afterwards, the fallout from the bomb attack had been swift and sure. The White House was evacuated and Frumpus had been taken to a secure location. All suspected clone infiltrators of the Cabinet had been rounded up and taken for thorough examination – for bomb implants – and then, no doubt, intensive questioning. There had been no more time for subtlety. The gloves had come off the paws. Distillery and her network had played their paw, and now it was time to make moves.

The impeachment of Presidog Frumpus had to be postponed as the White House government had unleased an emergency Executive Order and Martial Law had been declared. The Frumpus government was now on a war footing. Captain Podenko had explained *almost* everything to the Presidog. Those outside of the 'need to know,' did not know about the QA organization. As far as they were concerned, General Errol was a regular 5-Star US military officer. Yet there were others deep within the US military who *did know.*

Frumpus was a little miffed to find out that the real enemy was not Presidog Glutin and the Rushindogs. He was even more miffed when he was told that the real enemy was supposedly one of their own.

Frumpus tapped his chin. "Distillery Rodbottom? I know she's a bit of a witch but…a malicious mastermind of a smuggling cartel? Now that staggers belief. Not that I have much belief. Well, I guess anything goes really. If I can be Presidog of the United States of Ameridog, then anything is possible. After all, this is the land of the brave and the rich."

"Yes, Sir." Vice Presidog Spencer was becoming increasingly nervous at how events were turning out. To tell the truth, he had considered on several occasions to offer his resignation. Yet something kept niggling him to remain. And that niggling was the secret hope that one day Frumpus would do something silly, such as getting himself impeached, and then he could take over as Presidog. At one time he even harbored the thought of organizing an inside coup and snatching the Presidog position away from Frumpus. Then he would be top dog at the White House. But he just didn't have the testicles to do a thing like that. He was, in the end, a lap dog rather than a top dog.

It was Captain Podenko who was now taking charge of the situation. The political top dogs were safely in their secure location. He would leave Presidog Frumpus and Vice Presidog Spencer together to sort out the prattle of politics. Britdog agents Wag and Scally were now participating with Podenko and the rest of the military boys.

Scally sniffed the air. "Wag, are you wearing a musk perfume?"

Wag winced, as if offended. "Nah, dude, I don't wear perfume. That's for pansies, perverts, and entrepreneurs. What you're sniffing is my *male scent*. Mine is musky. That's my body armor odor sweat.

I'm all geared up for the revolution. What's your male scent?"

Scally shrugged. He had no idea. At least his shoulder had stopped hurting from Wag's fall. Wag leaned forward and took a long, deep whiff of his buddy.

"Mm…Jasmin," he said. "Not exactly gung-ho and hairy nipple. But it's got a kind of stealth quality to it, like a night raid."

"Good to know," said Scally. Wag never ceased to amaze him.

The raid of Distillery's home headquarters was back on. They'd had reports that she was last seen entering her Edgewater Ranch by the Lake Eerie. They couldn't be sure for how much longer she would remain there. They had to strike fast. They also reasoned that they needed to go in as soon as possible before Distillery and her staff could destroy any records they had. A night raid was planned – at 03.00 hours.

Wag and Scally had returned to their safe house to get some rest. Podenko had dispatched an armed officer to be stationed with them. His name was Randy Duke, and he was about as Ameridog as an Ameridog could be.

"Hey Randy, buddy," said Wag in one of his best Britdog accents, "did you know that if a dog's paw is as big as his face, then he's genetically smarter than other dogs?"

"Yeah?" Randy put his large paw up close to his face, just as Wag leaned over and gave Randy's paw a big push right smack into his nose. "Awwhhhh," bawled Randy.

Scally shook his head. "That's an old one, Wag."

"Old for us maybe, but new for testosterone Randy here." Wag grinned.

Scally decided it was the moment to check in back home one last time before the next morning's raid. He rang Dog Intelligence head office on his private phone.

"Hello, Epiphany dear, can you pass me onto *W*? I know, I should have rung the office more often. Heavy-duty stuff going down over here. What? Noo, I haven't been chasing the Ameridog girls – that's Wag's thing."

Wag looked up and shook his head. Scally didn't have a cat's chance in hell with Epiphany.

"Look, Epiphany, I'll bring you back something extra nice from the States. What? No, I promise it won't be a pair of dungarees. That's not fitting for a lady like yourself. You're as sweet as a..."

"I'm as sweet as a *what*, Agent Scally?"

"Ah, *W*, glad to have gotten hold of you." Epiphany had done it again, thought Scally. She was always catching him out. "I'm checking in with you before our raid tomorrow. Did you find out anything on Commander Thursday Adams and her sister, Tuesday – the CIA agents?" Scally listened attentively. He nodded his head a few times. "Uh-hu. Uh-hu. Got you. I understand. Yes, I'll check in again on the other side. Yes, agreed. I will. Thanks *W*."

"What and what?" asked Wag. "And what did we agree on?"

"We've agreed to take a voluntarily-forced vacation when this is over. And I also agreed to tell you."

Wag sighed. "Vacations are for normies who just live to die."

"I know, Wag, I know."

"Anything else – anything on Tuesday and Thursday?"

"Yes and no."

Wag listened to what Scally had to tell him as he made them both mugs of tea. He agreed, after listening, that things just didn't seem to make sense.

01.00 – Everyone was on route to Lake Eerie. First, they were to travel by helicopter so they could cover the ground quicker. Then they would be dropped in a field around twenty kilometers from the ranch where a set of vehicles would be waiting for them. They didn't want to take any chances by arriving too close by helicopter. Three blacked-out, non-registered helicopters swept through the night air. There was an unsettling feeling in the atmosphere. It was heavy as if a storm was brewing or as if electricity was congealing ready for a lightning blitz.

By 02.30 everyone was in place and positioned around the ranch. Wag had wondered why they had chosen 03.00 as the hour of the strike. Scally had said that it was the perfect witching time when night forces were the most powerful. But that had all sounded very occult to Wag. In the end, he guessed it was because three a.m. was when everyone would be in deepest sleep and dreaming of turtles.

"Why turtles?" asked Scally.

"What?"

"You were mumbling to yourself again. Something about dreaming of turtles."

"Ah, it's just the little demon I have in my head. He feeds me bad lines sometimes," replied Wag. He then made a note to self to not mumble out loud in future. And especially not just before a night raid.

The perimeter of Edgewater Ranch was secured with high-voltage fencing and movement-sensors. The first wave of the raid consisted of a specialist team to deactivate the perimeter security. Captain Podenko had confirmed to Wag and Scally previously that they'd been surveying this ranch by satellite for quite some time. They had acquired a very thorough plan of the ranch layout and had detected its security systems. There was a high suspicion that Distillery had installed some of the latest state-of-the-art electromagnetic, psychotronic, sonic, laser, and high intensity directed acoustics weaponry systems to protect the ranch. Of course, such weapons systems did not 'officially exist,' Podenko had said. But that didn't stop anyone from the top elite and wealthy from acquiring them from black military sources. That had made complete revolutionary sense to Wag. After all, the whole world had slipped into barking-dog madness. Scally had said that sanity is one of the rarest commodities on the planet – and Wag had to agree with that, one way or another (excluding the little demon in his head).

Right now, though, they were lying low in damp grass looking at one of the most highly secured private dwellings in the United States of Ameridog. It was even more secure than the Congress building at Capital Hill had been. Suddenly, they heard a low squeal. Shortly afterwards came the smell of burnt flesh. Podenko was speaking low through his walkie-talkie. He shook his head. One of the guys had just been electrocuted on the perimeter fence.

"Hey, look. Why don't you take a few guys and go back with the vehicles to the field, pick up the helicopters, and come back with an arial raid?" asked Scally.

Captain Podenko frowned. "Then it wouldn't exactly be a stealth raid, would it?"

"Any more fried soldiers and the ranch will be waking up to have a hot-dog barbeque breakfast," added Wag.

Scally agreed. "Stealth is good when it's done well. That's what the Britdogs do best. That's why they call our elite military the *Featherdogs* – they go in light as a feather. But you know what we privately call the US military? We call them the *WhamBang Boys*. You're best at going in, wham 'em and bang 'em up."

Podenko thought for a few seconds. He knew they had a point, even if he didn't wish to admit it.

"Think about it, buddy. Me and my pal here are going to take a waz. Don't wait for us." Wag nodded to Scally to follow him.

"A waz?" Podenko looked confused.

"Yeah. You know, like drain my pipe; shake hands with Wally; knock the dew off the lily; jimmy tiddle; bleed the lizard; syphon the python…"

"Okay, Wag. I think he got it. Let's go."

Wag and Scally stealth trotted back over the small hill behind them. Wag had a plan. In fact, it wasn't exactly his own plan so he couldn't take full credit for it. It was his little demon's plan. It had been whispered to him quietly in his head as he smelt the hot dog burnt flesh. And as the wise Lo-Poo says, remembered Wag: *the best way forward is not to do what others are doing.*

Fifteen minutes later and they were pushing away from the shore of the lake in a stolen wooden rowboat. Since it was Wag's idea, Scally had said, it would be best for him to do the rowing. Scally would concern himself with navigation. Wag smelt that jasmine male scent again – yes, Scally was seductive and stealthy. Onward they went at a rowing pace. They were guiding themselves by the light of the half moon. The night was eerily quiet, and the lake was calm. In the distance they could see the lights of the landing dock for Distillery's ranch. Why bother with the perimeter fence when you can row right up to the place from the lake? That had been Wag's little demonic contribution. It was Occam's Razor really – the simplest explanation is usually the right one.

As they got nearer to the landing dock, they both realized that just walking out of the boat and onto the decking may not be the wisest move.

"What was it you said about our military elite – they're the *Featherdogs*?" Wag looked over at his buddy.

Scally smiled in the moonlight. His cheeky Yorkshire terrier grin could melt a rhumba of rattlesnakes. "Sure was," he replied.

"Well, in this case, the *Featherdogs* are going to be the *Wetdogs*," said Wag. "We need to get into the water." Wag stopped rowing and looked over the side of the boat into the deep darkness of the water below. "I propose doggy paddle. You?"

Scally frowned. "Well, I'm certainly not going to be doing the butterfly."

They carefully lowered themselves into the cold water of Lake Eerie. The water didn't feel clean. In fact, it felt somewhat slimy as if filled with globulus algae. They both pulled a yukky face and then started to swim towards the landing deck.

"Do you think there's any turtles in here?" asked Wag, a tad concerned. He was beginning to think that he might be contracting a turtle phobia.

"There's always turtles, all the way down," replied Scally.

Wag didn't try to look down, not that he would be able to see much anyway. He swam even faster. A Britdog agent's natural terrain was dry land, not wishy-washy water, thought Wag, as he pulled himself up onto the wooden structure beneath the decking. His fur and paws felt greasy from the water. Scally scampered up behind him, agile and quick. Then again, he was the smaller and nimbler of the two.

Rather than climb up to the top, they decided to scramble through the under-decking to reach the shore, to keep out of sight from any surveillance cameras. They didn't want to be seen. Not yet. The first part of the plan was more stealth-like. And the second part. Well, they hadn't yet gotten to the second part. They were going to cross that bridge when they came to it, in true Wag and Scally style. Then…

Whoosh… Whoosh… Whoosh…

Three blacked-out helicopters flew low overhead.

"The *WhamBang Boys* have arrived," said Scally with a slight note of irony.

"We better screw the stealth for now then," added Wag.

On that they both agreed. And they were right. Sirens suddenly began wailing as the ranch security kicked into activation. Huge searchlights came on and started scanning the property. Captain Podenko's elite officers were sliding down ropes from the helicopters and were now on the ground. Another wave of trained US commandos came in on foot from the perimeter.

"Show time," said Scally, as he prepared for action.

"Hot dog time," mumbled Wag as he adjusted a cloth bandana around his head and then checked the equipment belt around his stocky waistline.

"You know what our plan is, right?" Scally

gave his buddy a questioning look.

"Sure thing. We search for Tuesday and Thursday. If we find them, we retrieve and get out fast. We leave Distillery and her gang for Podenko's boys."

Paw thumbs up.

Keeping low to the ground, Wag and Scally scampered over the grassy incline that led up from the lake edge. They wanted ranch security to keep all attention onto the incoming US dog soldiers. Those guys were sticking out like pink marshmallows at a white pajama party. Soon enough, broad-shouldered security goons came springing out from the main ranch building and firing madly into the night against all intruders. The spotlights were swinging from left to right trying to catch sight of their targets. Sirens were wailing, cats were screeching (oddly enough), and orders were being barked over the bedlam.

If Distillery does not know by now that she's being raided, then she's either on drugs or dead, thought Scally. He and Wag slipped around the side of the main ranch building, looking for an alternative way in. Only the *WhamBang Boys* use the front door. Civilized agents like Wag and Scally find a more diplomatic and subtle way to enter. That is, by not making a full-frontal entry.

Wag used his elbow to smash through a small ground floor window. He untied the bandana from his elbow and wrapped it around his head again. Wag looked back at Scally and shrugged. "Always works in the movies too." He then knocked out the remaining shards of glass and crawled through. Scally followed. They were in a large, marble-tiled bathroom. In one corner was a huge bath with so many taps attached to it that it appeared to serve as some type of triple jacuzzi-come-spa-douche machine.

"Afterwards, Wag," whispered Scally, noticing his buddy's curious stare. "First, we accomplish the mission – then we get lathered."

Scally peered through the door. A corridor led away with several other closed doors on either side. In the distance he could hear shouts and the sound of running. Outside, the gunshots and sirens continued. Scally knew that the US military soldiers had not yet penetrated the house. They were being held back, for now. Yet he had seen several of the US commandos drop onto the roof from one of the helicopters. They'd be making their way inside and could appear any minute. Scally led the way down the corridor and stopped abruptly as it opened out into a large salon. From the other side of the salon, it looked as if several staff members were huddled together, shaking, and scared. Within a few seconds, Scally had darted over, unseen, and was upon them.

He figured he didn't need to threaten them with a weapon as they were scared enough.

He grabbed one of them by the arm. "Follow me," he said. The group of four domestic staff ran quickly with Scally until he had taken them back to the marble bathroom. "Lock the door and stay here. Do you know if two Golden Labrador sisters are here? Their names are Thursday and Tuesday?"

One of them, a small Mexican Chihuahua, nodded her head. "Si, señor. Jueves and Martes are here. They stay with Gran Dama."

"Where?"

The Chihuahua pointed upwards.

"They're upstairs then?"

"Si, señor. But now they maybe not upstairs."

Scally frowned. "Then where would they be?"

The Chihuahua point downwards.

Wag grunted. "About as clear as government policy. It's either up or down." Then Wag thought a little. Mostly in movies everyone escaped by going upwards. Usually, that is, until they reached the roof and then there's nowhere else to go. But they were dealing with Distillery.

"Scally, let's go down. All heavy rocks fall downwards."

That sounded reasonable enough to Scally. "Señorita," he said, "show us downwards. Take us to the stairs."

Wag and Scally followed the small Mexican Chihuahua as she scurried along the corridors of the house. At one point they ran into three of Podenko's boys all dressed in military gear, with helmets and digital eye pieces. They quickly showed their special ID before they almost got knocked to the floor.

"Jeeezz, those dudes are like machines," muttered Wag. "Damn mini-terminators." Behind them they saw half a dozen other ranch members being rounded up and guarded by the US military in the middle of a room. Guns were pointing at their heads. Threats were being shouted. Wag wanted to go over and get the US boys to ease off a little.

Scally nudged him. "Come on, Wag. Stay on our objective."

The Chihuahua took them to a flight of steps. She pointed downwards and then put her little paw before her mouth as if to keep shush.

"Don't worry, señorita," whispered Scally. "We won't say a thing. Muchas gracias." He started down the steps cautiously.

Wag nodded to the Chihuahua. "Mucho thank-o," he said before following Scally. At the bottom of the stairs was a locked door. Wag remembered a saying from his favorite philosopher, the wise Lo-Poo: *The way ahead is only closed until you open it yourself.* Wag took some tools from his equipment belt and fiddled with the lock. He was going to open this door by himself, or his name was not Waginsky F. Jones. He fiddled and fiddled. There, he nearly had it. Just a final touch needed.

"Hey buddy, let me see your new US pistol." Scally handed it over. Wag fired at the door lock. "There – got it. Damn lock was a Japanese model."

A large, low-lit subterranean room stretched in front of them. On one side of the room, along the wall, were a series of glass cabinets. Wag stepped over and stared through the glass.

He immediately jerked back. "Whooah… heavy duty."

Inside the glass cabinets were duplicate copies of Nil Jiffyson. The clone bodies were strapped to machines with tubes going in and out, keeping them alive. Further along, behind drawn curtains, were several operating tables. Upon two of the tables lay a Nil Jiffyson cloned body that had been cut open as if part of a medical experiment.

"Maybe they were making more Nil Jiffyson bomb clones," said Scally, feeling disgusted at the thought of it.

"Or doing some weird type of genetic experiments," added Wag. He went behind one of the curtains to examine the body closer. As he did so, he heard a noise. There was a muffled voice, then the sound of a door being unlocked from down the hall. Scally was in full exposure in the middle of the room as Tuesday and Thursday entered. The two CIA agents stopped in their tracks. A look of surprise fell upon their faces.

"Scally?!"

"Thursday! Yes, it's me."

"Where's Wag?" asked Tuesday.

"He's coming," replied Scally, lying. "Before he does, you both better explain to me what's going on with you."

Thursday raised her gun and pointed it at Scally. "Nothing's going on with us. We are who we've always been."

"Not so," said Scally. "I know about your past. I had you checked out by UK Dog Intelligence. There are no records of any agents Tuesday and Thursday Adams. But I do know that there is a record of the Adams sisters being orphaned when very young and taken into military custody."

"Oh, who's a clever boy then?" The tone of Thursday's voice sounded different, as if distant and separated.

Wag was listening, quietly hidden behind the curtain. He slowly and very carefully crouched to the floor and crawled under the bed. He then crawled to get under the next bed so he could be closer to the sisters. Scally took a step forward.

"Stay right there," demanded Thursday, still holding the gun directly at him. Scally knew that Wag would be making a move, so he wanted to keep all the attention onto him as long as possible.

"Come on, Thursday. It's me. I'm your favorite Scally." He could see a ripple of tension appear on Thursday's face. There was a struggle going on somewhere inside of her.

Tuesday stepped closer. "You're in our way now. We will need to take care of you."

"What, like giving me a wash and a nice massage?" Scally was stalling for time. Wag had now made it to the third bed, crawling as quietly as he possibly could. Soon, he would be ready to jump the sisters.

"You are a foreign agent – Britdog Agent Scally – and we cannot allow you to ruin our plans." Thursday kept holding the gun aimed straight at Scally.

Scally held out his paws. "Come on, we're all friends here. This is just a game. And someone's got you all messed up. I know that you were just a little pup when you were orphaned. It's not your fault what the military did to you. Did they get into your heads? Did they break your personality? Come on. We can work this out together. I know there's the *real* Thursday inside of you."

"Don't listen to him," said Tuesday, standing a few feet behind her sister. "He's trying to confuse you."

"Sisters," said Scally, a little more forcefully now. "We don't need to do this. *You* don't need to do this. This is *not* who you really are. I know it's you, Thursday, inside of there. Listen to me – please!"

"No more!" shouted Tuesday. "Sis, remember the present, not the past."

Wag crouched down on all fours. He needed to make a distraction before he could get out from under the bed and do his famous ninja leap. What would they do in the movies? He thought quick and hard. Ah, yes, of course. He took a metal ball-bearing from his equipment belt. He had always wondered why Pavlov, the science director at Dog Intelligence, insisted on putting metal ball-bearings in an equipment belt. Now he knew why. It was obvious when you thought about it. Wag rolled the ball-bearing across the floor. It passed the feet of Tuesday and Thursday and continued rolling. Both ladies looked down. That was Scally's cue. He stepped forward just as Wag rushed out from under the bed and ninja leapt through the air to kick Tuesday squarely in the neck. Tuesday fell to the floor stunned just as the gun was fired. Wag suddenly turned to see Scally being jolted into the air and landing several feet away. Wag instinctively jumped at Thursday before she could turn around and he jabbed her with his tazer. Her whole body shook as she collapsed to the floor. Thursday wriggled further, trying to get back to her gun. Wag kicked the gun away and gave her another electroshock with the tazer. He noticed that Tuesday was trying to get up from the floor.

Quickly, he jumped on her and flattened her face down to the floor. Grabbing her paws behind her back he took a zip-tie from his belt and tightened it around Tuesday's paws. He went back and did the same with Thursday, retrieving his tazer. Then he ran over to where Scally lay. His buddy's body was covered in blood.

Scally looked up at Wag. "Have you got the girls?"

Wag nodded.

"Are they okay?"

"They'll be okay. Don't worry about them."

"And…and Distillery?"

"Don't worry about her. Remember, we stick to the plan. We're here to find and retrieve Tuesday and Thursday. We got what we came for," said Wag. They had found what was most important for them.

Wag turned again to his buddy. Taking from his equipment belt a medical patch, he unfolded it and pressed it against the bullet wound. "Now I know why you prefer scarlet waistcoats," he said, looking into Scally's face. "They hide the blood stains better."

Scally tried to laugh. But it hurt terribly to do so.

There was an unexpected acidic laugh from behind. Wag turned around. Before him stood a snarling

American Pit Bull Terrier. Distillery was dressed in tight black leather. It didn't suit her one little bit. Wag had to blink just in case he was having a hallucination. Saliva was dripping from her mouth.

"You're all cretins. All of you!" she said with a sneer. "And at least one of you is going to be tasting death this night."

Wag stood up. "You'll soon be tasting your own death. I'm not afraid of a bad breed like you. You think you're a mean mother hubbard, papa-one-eyed-jack. But you're just a walking grease ball."

Distillery pulled a face. She wasn't sure what to make of the Britdog insult. It was kind of surreal. "Your words are pitiful. All you morons are going to die out soon enough. We're going to have a de-population of moron dogs in this world, and then there'll be more room for us elite. We don't want to share this world with you useless eaters."
Wag had heard enough. It was time to take her out, even if she was one of the nastiest breeds to have to come face-to-face with. He took a step forward.

"A few more seconds and your friend will be dead. He got shot with a poisoned bullet. So, make your choice. Come for me or try to save your buddy. Time's ticking."

Wag swung around and dashed back to where Scally lay slumped on the floor. He ripped open his shirt. "Sorry, buddy. We'll get you a new one."

Finding where the bullet had entered the body, Wag pressed his lips against the wound and sucked. He spat out the first mouthful of blood. He sucked again – and spat out. He sucked again.

He didn't even hear Distillery leave. But Wag didn't care.

CHAPTER FOURTEEN

A Little Change of Mind

At the far end of Lake Eerie, Podenko's team eventually found Distillery's discarded mini submarine. What form of transport she had taken after leaving the submarine was anyone's guess. She had disappeared completely. Distillery Rodbottom had gone dark, no doubt hiding deep within her secret network.

"She won't leave the United States," said Captain Podenko. But he wasn't a hundred percent sure about that. Deep State rogues had a way of being protected by their own kind. They had tried to bring about the downfall of Presidog Frumpus and his Cabinet, first by infiltration to persuade him into war with the Rushindogs. And then by political impeachment.

Vice Presidog Spencer was relieved that the whole affair was over. It just meant that the animosity and rivalry between the Republicdogs and Demodogs was worse than ever. The minimal trust they had between them previously had now slipped into minus figures. There was a lot of political re-building necessary. And Spencer was not sure if Frumpus was the top dog for this particular job. He had his doubts.

Presidog Frumpus pouted. He was only glad that the whole emergency kerfuffle was over. The impeachment had been thrown out of court and several of Distillery's closest allies had been rounded-up, including Pansy Ploppy, the House Barker of Ameridog Kennel of Representatives. Or rather, the *Ex*-House Barker of Ameridog Kennel of Representatives. Frumpus was installed back into the White House, although with only half a Cabinet. He needed to re-shuffle the Cabinet and get good, solid folks around him who he could trust. In the meantime, Captain Podenko had returned to his military headquarters to assess the gains, and losses, of the recent raid. And privately, he also needed to meet with the QA organization. They were in need of a new military head, since General Errol's unfortunate demise. As all too often happened in such circumstances, the losses appeared to outweigh the gains. Yet Podenko was adamant to remain upbeat about the whole affair. Distillery Rodbottom, the Washington D.C. lynchpin in the dark international puppy smuggling network, had been taken out. That was, he reflected, a major achievement. Now they needed to follow the rest of the evil tentacles of the occult octopus.

Wag looked down sadly at the newly planted flowers around the grave. Such collateral damage in politically motivated war games made his belly turn in a bad way. Why you? he asked himself quietly. He added a single purple dahlia flower onto the grave.

"Yes, it is sad. We are so sorry," said Scally as he also planted a dahlia upon the grave. "Dear señorita Chihuahua, may you rest in peace."

"And have lots of fun with the Great Dog in the sky," added Wag.
Scally bowed and then turned to slowly walk away, his arm in a shoulder sling. Wag hopped up alongside his buddy and was just about to slap him on the shoulder.

"Hey, watch it Wag. Your slaps will send me back into the infirmary."

Wag laughed. "Good job the United Kingdog agreed to offer special agent medical cover otherwise the doctors here wouldn't have treated you."

"Tell me about it!" Scally automatically shrugged, and a jolt of pain shot through his shoulder. He guessed he didn't need Wag after all to induce some pain. "That damn *Bo-Ma Care* medical insurance is about as fair as a fencing match between flipperless fish."

Wag nodded. He didn't understand the analogy, but he could agree with the sentiment.

"Well, at least they cleaned your wound and stitched you back up again. Kinda lucky, don't you think, that the bullet hit the same shoulder implant that you had put in after your previous gunshot wound?"

"Yeah. Well, I did get the shoulder implant magnetized. Maybe that's what attracted the bullet there instead of the gut."

"Or the face," replied Wag, smiling. "I don't think I could quite imagine my mate Scally with a different face."

"Maybe we'll be cloned soon enough anyway."

"Ohhhh…if they clone me, I'm going to commit harakiri just to annoy my clone." Wag laughed to himself.

Scally had to think about that one. He looked over at his old friend and partner and felt a wave of gratitude roll over him. "Hey, Wag old buddy, I didn't get a chance before to thank you for sucking out the poison. It was a great thing you did. And," he continued, "if anyone was ever going to suck my poison, I'd prefer it to be you."

"Sure thing, Scally. And I'm just grateful that the wound was in your shoulder and not in your butt!"

Both agents laughed out loud. To tell the truth, they

were both relieved the whole nasty Ameridog mess was over with…for now.

"Okay, shall we go and visit the girls?" asked Scally.

Wag nodded. "I think we should."

Back in the Oval Office of the White House, Presidog Frumpus was pleased with himself. He had just successfully fended off another nagging phone attack from his ex-wife, Ayewanna. He knew she was a feisty Cesky Fousek breed when he married her. But he had been younger then, and even fuller of self-delusion and ego. He was cured of that now, or so he thought. In these later twilight years, all he really wanted was several golf courses and a few tall buildings in his name. Oh, and a sweet pussycat such as Sueme, his Siamese lady friend.

Frumpus slurped on his diet cola, thinking of the old days with Ayewanna, and the more recent good times with Sueme. Why wasn't a dog's life easy, he thought? Simple things always ended up as complicated. And complicated things – well, they just couldn't be plain understood. He popped another jellybean in his mouth and chewed on it slowly, savoring the flavor as it crumbled in his mouth. Yes, nothing better than the red jellybeans. His mind wandered to the image of the beans that his grandmother used to plant in the garden. Or was it jellies? Yes, the jellyfish in the sea where they used to take summer vacations as a family. Nothing like family, he thought. He was once a baby, oh so long ago when cowboys were heroes and ray guns were cool. He was not such a baby now, although he did like jelly babies as well as jellybeans. They were tasty too. He wondered what the difference was between a jellybean and a jelly baby. He wasn't really sure. Maybe they should print on the packaging what the difference is. Surely, jellybean eaters and jelly baby eaters deserve to know the difference.

"Sir?" Vice Presidog Spencer interrupted Frumpus's important thoughts.

"Oh. Uh-hu? Yes, Spencer, what is it – another UFO sighting?"

"No, Sir. I have news about Pansy Ploppy."

"Ah yes, the ex-House Barker. What happened to her? We rounded up those Demodogs, didn't we? Did she resign to join a church choir, or something?"

"Yes, we did, Sir. And we gave them all medical checks to see if any of them were clones."

"And?" asked Frumpus, showing impatience.

"Yes, we got the clones, Sir. And it turned out that Pansy Ploppy was found to have dementia. A private court hearing decided that the best thing was to place her into a specialist home. Pansy now resides, without choice, at the Dogsanto Residence for Dementia, which is run by the Dogson & Dogson Pharmaceutical company and sponsored by the Dill

& Bellend Mates Foundation."

"Oh, good. That sounds great. I mean, the home. Shame about the dementia though. I guess it happens to the worst as well as to the best of us."

"Indeed, Sir. But rest assured, Pansy will be receiving the best medical attention. She'll be getting regular vaccinations and boosters to help her with the dementia."

"Splendid, Spencer. Splendid. Fancy a jellybean?"

Scally read the large name board at the entrance as they stepped out of the taxi. It read: **The Sidney Gotlip Center for Mind Reconditioning.** Neither Wag nor Scally said a word. They didn't need to.

Once inside the building and past the heavy security, they were ushered into the head doctor's office. They were asked to be seated until the doctor arrived. A name plaque on the desk read: *Donald 'Conan' Cameron.* Around the room were hung pictures of mountainous landscapes. Wag had his nose almost pressed against one of them when the doctor came in. He was a small, disheveled looking Scottish Border Terrier. His hair was unraveled, and he held a clipboard under one arm, exactly how you might expect a doctor to look. No surprises there then.

"Ah, the Scottish Highlands. That's where my heart roams. Good day, sirs, I am Doctor Cameron. I believe you are here about the CIA sisters, as we call them." He chuckled, although clearly to himself.

"We are," replied Scally in a soft yet firm voice. "They are our colleagues, and naturally we are concerned for their welfare."

"Naturally," replied the doctor, shuffling his papers, though more for the 'doctor effect' than anything else. "We are also a CIA-funded research institute. I must remind you that what happens at the Sidney Gotlip Center for Mind Reconditioning stays at the Sidney Gotlip Center for Mind Reconditioning. Agreed?"
Wag and Scally both nodded their heads, although only barely.

"Good. Now, I have been informed that you are special agents on behalf of the United Kingdog. Ah, makes me think back to the Scottish Highlands. That's where my heart roams – did I ever tell you that? Well, enough of myself. I don't wish to over-Scottish you with my own heritage. Yes, the CIA sisters. Let me see." The doctor pawed through the papers in front of him. "Sure. Yes. They were part of an experiment here when they were first brought to us. Yes, they were orphans then it says. They were placed in the **MC-MEGA** program, and from a very young age."

"They were orphaned when young, and the US military brought them here," said Scally, with an obvious tone of disdain.

"Quite so. Yes. And they were placed in the **MC-MEGA** program, as I have said, which was run by my predecessor, the illustrious Dr. Sidney Gotlip. They were one of the CIA's experiments, to create double agents through mind reprogramming. A masterful program to create agents that could also act as pretend double agents without them even knowing about it."

"What you mean to say is that you messed with their heads." said Wag, bitterly.

"In a round-about way, yes. Their minds were simply fragmented, decompartmentalized, and then put back together, with a tad or two of extra hidden information. They could then be used to infiltrate our enemies as double agents, and they wouldn't even know it. Marvelous stuff, really."

"Not from where we're sitting. And the sisters eventually became double agents that turned against yourselves, no?" Wag looked across at Scally and pulled a 'beam me out of here' face.

"Ah, yes. It seems that some other parties must have gotten to them also. Amazing to think that others out there know about this work and how to do this stuff. It appears that another layer of programming was put into their minds so that the sisters thought that they had been programmed as false CIA agents when in fact they were working for another organization. It's like an onion, you see, with layer after layer."

"The sisters are *not like onions*, doctor," said Scally annoyed.

"Right so. Right so. Well, we really are living at a time of crazy brain programming. Take for instance, television – now, there's a wonderful programming medium if ever I saw…"

"Thank you, doctor," interrupted Scally. "Can we just see Thursday and Tuesday?"

"It's a special agent thing. I'm sure you understand, Doc," added Wag, winking to the doctor.

Doctor Donald 'Conan' Cameron smiled back. "Sure. From one operative to another, I can understand these things."

The interior of the Sidney Gotlip Center for Mind Reconditioning was hygienic, bleak, and insipid. It was the kind of location that would fail to inspire a moron. The whole place felt lifeless, as if it existed as its own form of black hole, sucking all energy and light into itself. Wag and Scally were shown to a room by an equally bland and lifeless orderly. They opened the door and stepped through. Inside the private room were two beds, separated by a white curtain on rails. Wag grabbed the rails and swung it away. They didn't want any more curtains or dividers. In both beds lay an almost identical and very tired looking Golden Labrador, with soft brown eyes that could melt a renegade platoon of deranged sheep. In one bed lay Tuesday Adams; and in the other, Thursday Adams.

"Hello Thurs," said Scally, in a gentle voice.

"Hi Scal." Thursday smiled, although showing some discomfort, or perhaps embarrassment.

"I brought you something. I thought you might enjoy a little reading."

"Cool. What is it?"

Scally held up a book. "It's a book about finding one's true purpose in life. It's called *Meetings with Remarkable Dogs* by Dogjieff."

"Thanks, Scally. I'd love to read it." Thursday smiled and a spark of warmth lit her tired face.

"Hey Tuesday," said Wag.

"What's up, Wagamonster – or is it Waginsky?"

"It's whatever tickles your tummy, sweetie." Wag sat at the end of Tuesday's bed. "I got you something too. Maybe it will take your mind in a new direction." He held up a small paperback book. "It's called *Do Dog Clones Dream of Electric Cats* by Philip K. Dogdick."

"Mmm…topical," replied Tuesday.

Wag could see she was clearly impressed. "But you don't need to read it all at once. I wouldn't want it to stress your brain out too much, you know?" Scally, at the next bed, shook his head in disbelief.

Tuesday nodded. "I know that you're only

thinking of me, Wag. And I think I'll be alright from now on."

"Cool to hear it. So, did the Doc put all the pieces back together inside – back to how they were before you got screwed up?"

Tuesday laughed gently. "Yes, Wag. More or less back to before."

"Good, because I miss the way you flip your pancakes. Any other pancake just isn't the same." Wag grinned. Then his face turned serious, and he leaned forward to whisper. "Hey, when we were, you know, doggy smooching, was I with the real Tuesday or with the other psychopathic assassin part?"

"You were always with the real me," whispered back Tuesday.

"What was that?" asked Scally.

Wag looked over at his buddy. "Oh, just agent talk. You know, clone assassins, poisoned bullets, psychopathic politicians, and all that stuff."
Scally and Thursday both laughed.

"A little humor is a good cure for the ills of this world," said Thursday. "There's enough evil in the world already, and we can't play their game. It's no good to fight fire with fire. We need some heart stuff too."

On that, Scally had to agree. "And when you're feeling better," he added, "maybe you should both take a vacation. Get a little European sunshine into you."

Having the afternoon free, Wag and Scally decided it would be a good thing to share some more 'agent talk' with the Adams sisters. Jellybean-eating presidogs, undercover double agents in their governments, moon bases, moondogs, honey traps, and all the rest. You know, just the usual chit-chat between Britdog special agents and their ex-mind programmed CIA-controlled-gone-rogue counterparts. And the sun shone through the window and softly rested upon the room.

Later that evening, back at their original hotel room, Wag and Scally were both exhausted. Presidog Frumpus had invited them to an evening of bowling to say thanks for their help in how Frumpus had almost single-handedly thwarted an evil plan to ruin the government and start a war with the Rushindogs. Luckily, Frumpus had had the quick wits to save the day. But still, he wanted to say a little thanks to his Britdog agent buddies for offering their advice along the way. And it was also a good excuse to go bowling too.

Yet Wag and Scally had declined. They were too tired for any more shenanigans. Captain Podenko had rung them from a 'I-can't-tell-you-where-I-am' secret military location to offer his thanks and best wishes to them both.

The Ameridog night had turned pitch black, yet from the window of their hotel suite the lights of Washington D.C. could be seen like a sprinkle of deranged fireflies. Scally was looking out over the late evening skyline.

"You're thinking it would have been better if they had caught Distillery Rodbottom?" asked Wag.

Scally shrugged. "Mmm. I guess it would have been better. But in a way, I doubt it would have really changed things. Another devious dog would have taken her place, equally as immoral and psychotic. There's too many applicants for such a job, unfortunately."

"They're out there, and they keep on coming and coming," said Wag as he strolled over to the window and offered his buddy a mug of hot Britdog tea.

"Yeah. Keeps guys like us busy, I suppose. But there's something fundamentally wrong with this world and I just can't quite put my paw on it."

Wag slurped his tea. "It's an upside-down world, and we're one of the few standing the right way up."

"Maybe you're right, Wag. Maybe you're right."

"Hot dog, I am."

Scally's personal phone rang. He picked it up. It was *W* from Dog Intelligence.

"Scallan, are you going to get your lazy butts back over here or do I have to look for two more scallywags to take your place?" Scally closed the phone. It was far more interesting watching the deranged fireflies over Washington D.C.

CHAPTER FIFTEEN

The New Normal

There were many things to miss about the United Kingdog, but CCTV cameras and traffic were not included. Nor were over-zealous security, new dog distancing rules, and paw sanitizers.

Wag looked at the paw sanitizer. "You want me to squirt that goo onto my paws?"

Epiphany looked sympathetic. "It's the new regulations. They call it the 'new normal.' "

Wag breathed in deeply, paused, then exhaled slowly. "Sounds like a crock of poop to me. I'd rather expel the hamster live on TV than splash that chemical sluice on my paws."

"My dear Epiphany, we've only been away a short time, and so much has changed. The UK customs official even asked to see our rabies certificate," said Scally in as diplomatic a tone as possible.

"Yeah, lucky my black market one still works," added Wag, scratching his butt.

Epiphany gave them both a questioning look. "Scally, a world traveler like yourself has to get used to change. This is the new paradigm now."

Wag roared out in laughter. He couldn't stop himself. He bent forward and doubled up. "The new paradigm!! The new paradigm? What's thats then, more capitalism but greener, and with invented oxygen taxes?"

Epiphany shook her head. "Oh Wag, you're so uncensored."

The buzzer lit up on Epiphany's desk.

"You can both go in now. *W* is expecting you."

Scally bowed and handed her a little paper bag. "Here, my dear, a little memento for you."

Epiphany tried to hide her blush. She opened the bag. Inside was a 'I Love Washington D.C.' fridge magnet with a picture of the White House on it.

W the pug, Head of Dog Intelligence, was not too well pug-pleased – as usual. You could never be sure if she was frowning, scowling, or just looking straight ahead. A pug's face is wrinkled whether it is sneering or smiling, and no miracle wrinkle cream in the world could fix that.

"Another rainy day in the UK," said Scally in a casual tone of voice.

"This UK pug doesn't care about the bloody weather," replied *W*, as she leaned back in her high-top chair. "What the blazing belly-ass buffoonery went on in the US? I heard you had a few raids that went butt-up?"

Scally shrugged. "The Ameridog gung-ho boys were heavy handed. But we got a result, and Frumpus is happily on his throne again."

"And there's one less pizza restaurant in Washington," added Wag with a helpful smile.

"I heard from our intelligence that you broke up a puppy smuggling ring. Did you get the ringleaders?"

"The Washington D.C. ring is busted. That's the best for now. We didn't get the main top dog in Washington – Distillery Rodbottom – but it's safe to say we won't be hearing a peep from her for a while. She's gone into hiding."

W looked over the top of her desk at Scally. "You neither look nor sound convinced. Spit it out."

Scally inhaled loudly. More loudly that he wished as it almost sounded as if he was whistling.

"This thing is international. All we've done is burnt one of the tentacles. The full octopus is alive and well."

W banged her tiny yet powerful paw upon the desk. "Damn right it's alive and well. Whatever or whoever this squiggly octopus is, it's been rattling at my door and peeing on my floor. Can you imagine the hassle it's given me?"

Scally looked over at Wag with an innocent face. Wag, almost theatrically, pulled an innocent face back.

"No, you can't!" continued *W*. "Some high up bigwigs have been leaning on my bosses who've then been leaning on me. They want you guys fired - kerzip, outta here! They know you're getting close to the fire and that makes them feel the heat."

Scally looked thoughtful. "The whole system is polluted, *W*, and you know it."

W leaned forward and said, in a whisper - "you know it, I know it, the bleeding bathroom cleaner knows it. But it doesn't change the fact."

Wag turned around to walk away.

"And where do you think you're going, Wag?" asked *W* in her raised voice.

"I thought we were fired," replied Wag, nonchalantly.

"Don't be a wise-ass. I'm not firing you boys. You're the last thing we've got between here and bedlam. And besides, I don't take my orders from a bunch of paw-licking masonic moonshiners. You're staying here with me." *W* paused and took a breath.

"Well, not exactly here, right here. And not right now either. Take a break. Go somewhere. Lie low for a while. Out of sight and certainly out of trouble."

"You mean take a holiday?" asked Scally.

"And is it full paid?" asked Wag.

This time *W* really did scowl. "Don't push it. You'll get basic expenses covered, that's all. Now off you go. Have a break. Recharge your batteries. Do whatever you wish to do for a while – just ease off and lie low."

"Sure thing, boss." Scally smiled as he stroked his injured shoulder. He was actually thinking that a holiday would do him good.

"Chock-a-doobie," replied Wag with a lazy half-salute.
They both turned to walk out of the room.

"Oh, and by the way – thanks boys. You did well in Ameridog." *W* looked down and continued to shuffle through the papers on her desk as Wag closed the door behind them.

Epiphany watched them closely as they came back.

"You going away again, right?"

"Sorry kiddo," said Scally. "We've been taken off Dog Intelligence."

Epiphany looked surprised. "What for?!"

"For mockery of the system," interrupted Wag. "And for having too clean paws."

Epiphany didn't look convinced. "You'll be back," she said looking directly at Scally.

"Maybe." Scally went over to Epiphany, a beautiful and highly intelligent Pomeranian dog. He lifted his paw and gently touched her on the cheek. "Here's looking at you, kid." Then he walked away. Epiphany looked saddened.

"I hope he sanitized his paws before he touched you," added Wag as he too walked out.

The next day, after breakfast, Wag and Scally were all packed to go. They were only now waiting for the taxi to arrive. Wag had unzipped his large duffle bag and was rummaging through it.

"Wag, I hope you're not going to make us late." Scally looked on, impatiently.

"Nah. Just checking to see if I packed my Marmite."

"Come on, Wag. Where we're going you don't need Marmite," Scally said frustratingly.

"Look, dude. Marmite is my friend. Don't dis my friend. Ah, found it!" Wag zipped up his bag and tossed it over his shoulder. "Here, I'll drag your suitcase now that you're a wounded cripple."

"Thanks, buddy," replied Scally sarcastically. "But my shoulder wound is getting better. And my suitcase has wheels so I can drag it just fine."

"Suit yourself."

The taxi pulled up outside. The bags were loaded and soon they were away. In a couple of hours, they would be at the airport, and then…

"Going somewhere nice, fellas?" asked the taxi driver in the usual chatty way.

"Yes, we are," replied Scally, feeling relaxed. "We're heading for the European sunshine. Going to the Costa del Sol."

"Nice one, fellas."

Scally smiled to himself as he pulled out his newspaper and read the Thursday edition news. He was ready to take his mind off things for a while.

Wag sank back into his seat and pulled out a lollipop he had been saving just for an occasion like this. It was an orange-yellow mango flavored lollipop. He put on his headphones and flicked through the tracks on his phone. Ah yes, he found it. One of his favorite artists and just right for the moment. He clicked on Dog Morrison, and closed his eyes as the *Brown Eyed Girl* sang into his ears and warmed his doggy heart…

My brown-eyed girl
And you, my brown-eyed girl
And whatever happened
To Tuesday and so slow?

Going down the old mine with a
Transistor radio
Standing in the sunlight laughing
Hiding behind a rainbow's wall
Slipping and sliding
All along the waterfall with you
My brown-eyed girl
You, my brown-eyed girl

FIN!

My Motto:

te potest - aut erit aliquis
esti vi mem - aŭ esti iu alia

I'm friendly and uncooperative at the same time. People know me to be unbelievably ambiguous and imaginatively unbelievable. I don't consider myself to be either a paradox or a straight line. My beliefs are minimal and diminishing. My opinions are flexible and should not be trusted – believe me! People should take my word on not believing me totally. Total belief is a mirage, in my flexible opinion. That's about it for now, although there could be more to come. More on that later. See you all on the upside.

For more information, visit:

https://www.baronvondennis.com/